D0034494

The Turtle of Michigan

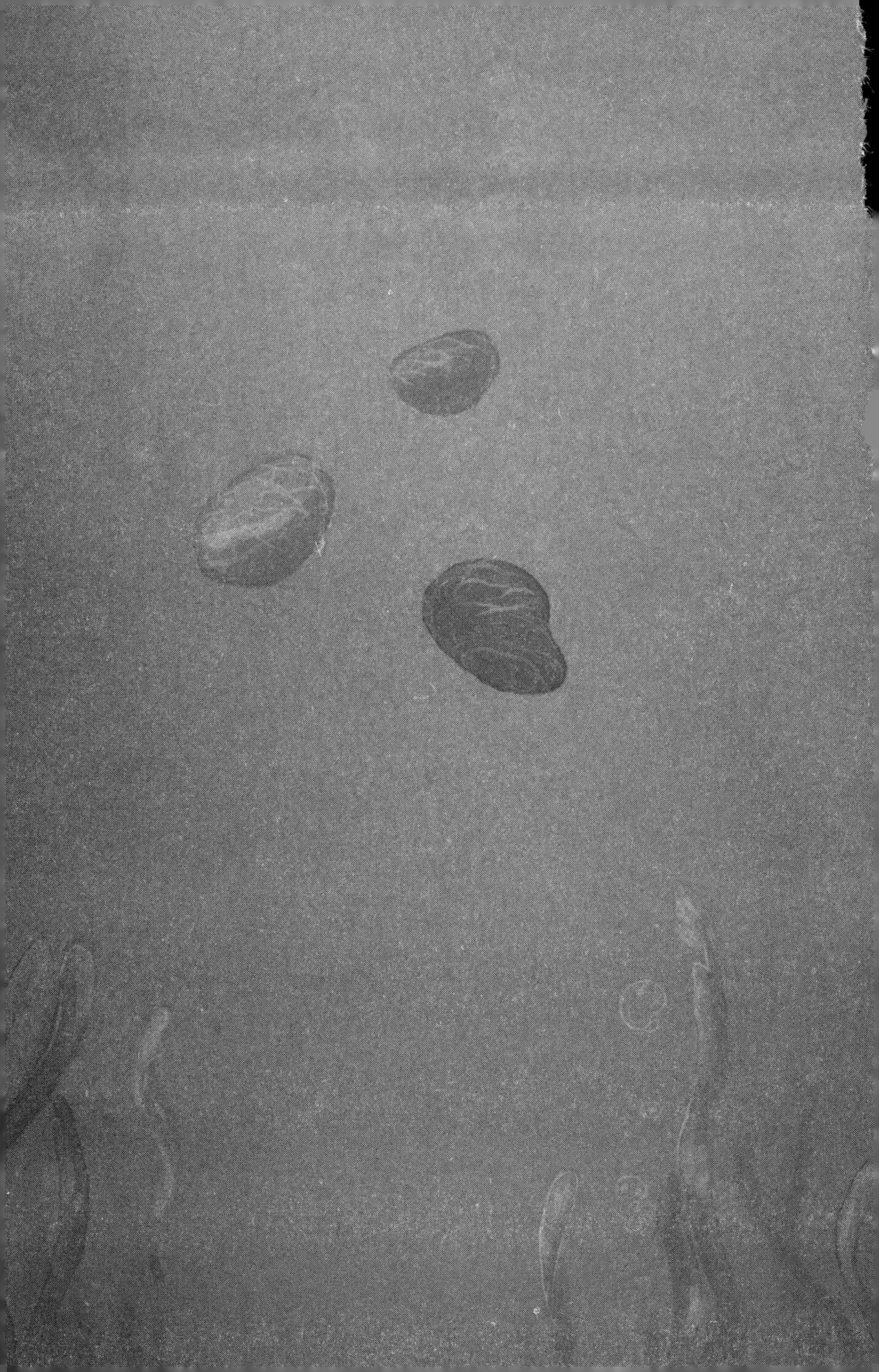

Naomi Shihab Nye

ILLUSTRATIONS BY

Betsy Peterschmidt

The Turtle of Michigan

a novel

GREENWILLOW BOOKS

An Imprint of HarperCollins*Publishers*

The Turtle of Michigan

 Printed in the United States of America. For information address HarperCollins Children's Books, a division of HarperCollins Publishers, 195 Broadway, New York, NY 10007.
www.harpercollinschildrens.com

The text of this book is set in 12-point ITC Espirit.
Book design by Paul Zakris

Library of Congress Cataloging-in-Publication Data

Names: Nye, Naomi Shihab, author.
Title: The turtle of Michigan / by Naomi Shihab Nye.
Description: First edition. | New York : Greenwillow Books, an Imprint of HarperCollins Publishers, [2022] | Audience: Ages 8–12. | Audience: Grades 4–6. | Summary: Eight-year-old Aref is excited to reunite with his father in Ann Arbor, Michigan, where he will start a new school, and while Aref misses his grandfather, his Sidi, he knows that his home in Oman will always be waiting for him.
Identifiers: LCCN 2021055302 (print) | LCCN 2021055303 (ebook) | ISBN 9780063014169 (hardcover) | ISBN 9780063014183 (ebook)
Subjects: CYAC: Emigration and immigration—Fiction. | Moving, Household—Fiction. | Family life—Fiction. | School—Fiction. | Michigan—Fiction. | Oman—Fiction. | LCGFT: Fiction.
Classification: LCC PZ7.N976 Tup 2022 (print) | LCC PZ7.N976 (ebook) | DDC [Fic]—dc23 LC record available at https://lccn.loc.gov/2021055302
LC ebook record available at https://lccn.loc.gov/2021055303

10 9 8 7 6 5 4 3 2
First Edition

Greenwillow Books

In respectful memory,
Sultan Qaboos bin Said Al Said (1940–2020)

Note:
Sidi is pronounced "See-Dee."
Aref is pronounced "R-F."

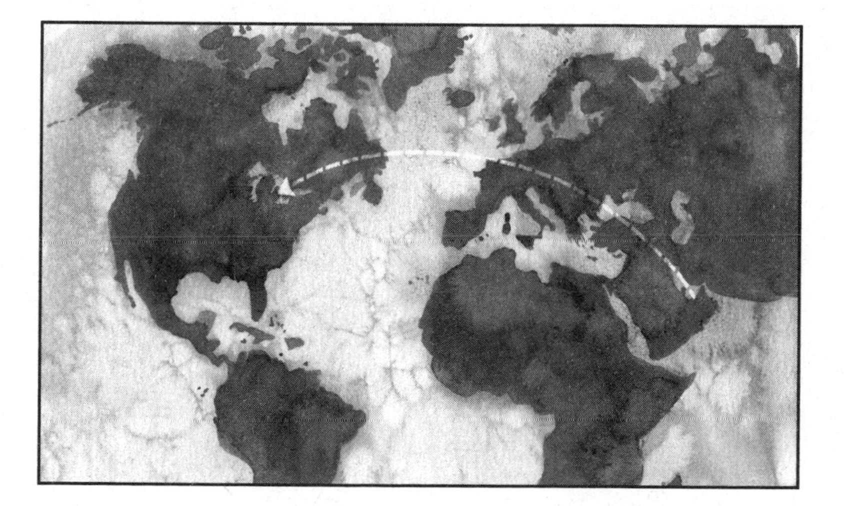

Bon Voyage!

The moment the giant silver jet took off from Muscat International Airport, wheels lifting from the runway, Aref Al-Amri started laughing. Shaking and giggling as if a strong wave had rolled up from inside of him, he was laughing hard in seat 14A!

"What is it, habibi?" his mother asked from the next seat. "What's the joke?"

He couldn't tell her. He didn't even know.

In the weeks and days leading up to this moment, he had felt worried, and mad. He wouldn't even pack his suitcase. The suitcase that right this minute was in the belly of the plane. He'd said to his grandfather, "Sidi, I am scared of everything. I don't want to go, and I think I won't like it."

He told his mom, "This is a very bad idea you made up for me."

He stomped his feet and banged a few doors.

He didn't want to move halfway around the world. What if no one liked him or even wanted to know him? People in other places already had their friends, and his friends were here in Oman. His brain felt stuck in a sad place the whole time they were preparing to leave.

And now he was laughing! Everything suddenly felt good!

Even walking down the airplane aisle and finding their big golden seats lined up with all the other seats so neatly felt like a pleasure. He had pushed his backpack under the seat in front of him and snuggled into position, rearranging his tightly latched seat belt. He stretched his legs out. He didn't feel crowded at all. He liked all the nifty buttons in the ceiling and on the armrest. He appreciated his air vent, blasting a strong current of air into his face. He was glad his seat was by the window.

Right when the roaring airplane engine revved loudly, and the wheels started rolling, and the plane tilted up into the sky, a little whisper tickled Aref from deep inside his mind. *Relief! Adventure!*

His spirits lit up, as if the fear had flown out of him.

But his mom was not laughing. Her eyes were tightly closed, hands gripped together in her lap. A tear was dripping down her cheek. She reached up to wipe it away.

"Mom!"

She didn't answer him. This was a surprise—she had seemed so happy to be going to the United States. Had they just traded personalities?

She reached over, gently touching his hair and shoulder, and tried to smile. But she kept her eyes closed while doing it.

He nudged her. "What's wrong?"

"It's a new chapter, my love," she said. "I will miss our country, too, you know. You're not the only one."

And then something weird happened. Her own words came out of his mouth.

"Remember, we'll be back," Aref said. "It's just for a short time." He felt like an echo. This was exactly what she had been saying to him for weeks and weeks!

His mom smiled. She whispered, "Bon voyage"—"good journey" in French. She didn't really speak French; she just knew a few words in different languages since she was an English teacher and loved words. "Merci, Madame," said Aref, proud that he knew that much. Everyone always told him he was lucky to be so fluent in English and Arabic both. "Well, my mom's an English teacher," he always said. "And my school speaks English."

* * *

Outside in the big darkness, the giant tipped sliver of a crescent moon was rising over Muscat—the same quiet moon he and Sidi had watched from Sidi's roof when they slept up there last week. Their old friend, the moon. But looking so different now. Still, it was fine. The moon knew how to change, but always be present. Sidi had told Aref that the moon would be with him everywhere. This was helpful. This would be one of the secret thoughts that helped him get through.

The Hand

When you were in an airplane, none of your land worries seemed big at all. You forgot what you worried about in the first place. You couldn't see the hospital with its lit-up windows or the parking lots crowded with traffic or the sad house whose water heater blew the roof off. You were bigger than the biggest bird, holding power inside you.

Anything could happen. Soon you had a

little bag of crackers in your lap, and someone was asking if you wanted apple juice.

They were flying to Paris, then to New York City, then to Detroit, Michigan. Aref's father would pick them up at the Detroit airport in a car he was renting until they got their own car, and they would drive to Ann Arbor, not too far away. Aref and his mother would see their new apartment for the first time.

Aref really loved names of cities. He spent hours staring at maps, memorizing them. *Seeb! Kalamazoo! Honolulu! Sandwich! Toad Suck!* So he liked staring at his own plane tickets, seeing his name printed above the name of a different place. He liked focusing on the map in the airline magazine, soaking up some new names. He hadn't known before that airplanes had magazines.

It felt odd to fly in an airplane at night, at the same time you were usually putting on your pajamas and going to bed. Tonight Aref would not have to go to bed. They would push the levers on the sides of their seats and tip back a little. Each comfy seat contained a pillow in a fresh cover, like an envelope, and a dark-blue blanket in a plastic sack.

"This is a great TV screen!" Aref was whispering to himself. He could click his own remote control and watch shows once they started flying. His friend Riyad had told him that he had watched four movies in a row on the way to New York. There were Disney movies, cartoons, zombies, and games. Aref could watch TV all night if his mom kept her eyes closed. She wouldn't see what he chose. She wouldn't tell him to turn it off.

* * *

The lights of Muscat dimmed beneath the plane. All the beautiful beige and white buildings were smaller than little toys that could get lost under the bed. The purple blue-brown mountains behind the city shrank away, too; even their shadows were gone. Everything was so small. Everything was the same size.

Apartments and houses, schools and parks, the big grocery stores and the tiny Thai restaurants, the open market and beautiful library, Sidi's old sandal shop, big and little roads, bridges and soccer fields, hotels and beaches—you flew over all of them.

But where was Sidi's house?

Aref hadn't been able to see Sidi's neighborhood at all. He couldn't pick out any specific neighborhoods in all that darkness. Sidi

had said he would be standing on the roof waving. He had promised. Was he there?

Good-bye to everything Aref ever knew! The plane rose gracefully into the world of clouds and cloud stories, those drifting tales Sidi always told. Aref and his mother were joining the higher air of falcons, then flying above the falcons. The sky was very giant, very wide. Aref felt bigger already. He sat up tall in his seat and looked around.

One thing he had noticed at the gate before getting on the airplane was that there weren't many kids on this flight. Mostly there were sunburned tourist-looking people and businesspeople in dark suits and maybe some deep-sea divers and ship captains and librarians and some people from India and a few women maybe from Saudi Arabia

wearing hijabs and their husbands or fathers or grandfathers, and only one other kid around his age. She had a blond ponytail with a puffy pink twist holding it together. He'd walked over to her bravely and said, "Hello!" She smiled but didn't answer. Then he said, "Marhaba!" in case she spoke Arabic, not English. She still didn't answer. Now, though, he noticed she was sitting right in front of him! He quickly slid back down in his seat.

But as soon as the plane leveled out, after tipping upward like a rocket launching, something incredible happened. The girl stuck her hand back between the seat and the side of the plane, under the window, toward him. *What was she doing?* Aref stared at her pale hand. Her wrist wore a little pink and yellow bracelet made of strings braided

together. He looked at his mom. Her eyes were still closed. She seemed to have fallen asleep already. So Aref reached out and touched the girl's hand. At first he tried to shake it, like grown-ups meeting, but she wrapped her fingers around his own and held on tightly. His heart pounded. They flew this way for a few minutes before she let go and pulled her hand back.

He couldn't see the girl's face. She hadn't answered him when he tried to say hello at the gate. But even in the cold blast from the vent, he felt a warm glow in his cheeks. Aref had a friend on the airplane. They didn't speak the same language, but they were sharing a ride.

Friends You Never Dream Of

The engine settled down from its biggest roar and began humming. It was a nice, comfortable sound, like ten air conditioners turned on softly at once.

A tall flight attendant wearing a red beret leaned over Aref's mother and said to Aref, "Is this your first flight?"

Surprised, he nodded.

"Would you like to meet the captain?" she asked.

Meet the captain? What was she talking about?

"Undo your seat belt and walk to the cockpit with me," she said, smiling.

Walk to the cockpit? Seriously? Aref needed to tell this to Sidi!

He snapped his seat belt open and scrambled over his drowsy mom's legs. She opened her eyes a crack, saw the attendant beckoning him, and nodded. "Go ahead, habibi."

The flight attendant paused at the row in front of Aref's and said to the girl's mother, "Excuse me, is this her first flight?"

"No! Colette, she fly more times," the other mom said.

So now Aref knew the girl's name. *Colette.*

Colette didn't get to go to the cockpit then. She smiled at him, though.

* * *

The cockpit was full of one thousand buttons, levers, numbers, dials, graphs, tiny windows, and bright lights, some white, some green, some blinking. There were three pilots up there, actually: a captain wearing headphones, a copilot, and an extra pilot, who handed Aref a pin of golden wings and a piece of paper declaring him a first-time flyer with the details filled in about their trip, Muscat to Paris, and a place to write his own name, with the date. The captain had already signed it. Wow! It was a document of proof.

"Are you having a good time?" the pilot asked him.

"Great!" said Aref.

The pilot helped Aref pin the wings on his

denim jacket. He patted his shoulder. "We are glad you are flying with us tonight. Welcome to the skies."

Aref walked back to his seat shining like a sunbeam, thinking *I could be a pilot*, something he had never thought before, not even once. He noticed that many of the passengers were wrapped in their blankets like mummies, slouched in their seats, wearing dark blue eye masks. How could they sleep at a thrilling time like this?

Soon Aref was eating pasta with tomato sauce and mushrooms. He liked the food tray with its small round bread bun and tiny salt and pepper packets. He liked the miniature salad and the brownie for dessert. After he finished, he watched French cartoons with cats swinging on ropes from the ceiling of

a giant castle, then ripped the plastic sack around his own blanket open. He tucked it under his chin and leaned back.

Aref dreamed of odd things in Muscat he wouldn't see for three years—the intricate balconies on buildings in Muttrah, the glass faces of newer buildings up toward the hills, the way they shone an unearthly green light at sundown. The golden fields on the edge of Muscat, right before the desert and mountains, after the houses stopped; the way they stretched open and he wanted to run through them. The graceful big gate over the road by the sea. The dome and towers of the Sultan Qaboos Grand Mosque lit up and glittering like one of the world's wonders. He dreamed about the way Sidi cut a cantaloupe, neat

triangles and chunks, and scooped the seeds away. He dreamed of his soft, cozy bed and missed it. He dreamed of Mish-Mish, his cat, jumping high into the air and doing a backflip when he gave her some catnip.

Sidi's Secret Thoughts, Not Told, Not Written

He is really gone now.

He will be gone a long time.

I told him it was not long,

but I was just

trying

to make him feel better.

Paris Airport

When they exited the plane in Paris, Colette turned and waved to him. He waved back. Then she disappeared with her parents forever into a crowd. Aref wished she had not disappeared. *We never spoke one word, but I might remember her,* he thought.

His body felt weird and stiff. It was hard to sleep on a plane. He wished they were there already, but they still had a very long way to

go. His mom seemed anxious, searching for the right gate for the flight to New York City. The airport loomed huge and gray around them, full of moving sidewalks and tired-looking travelers. Was it morning here? It was hard to tell what time it was. Aref pulled his small carry-on suitcase with a blue whale on it. He also wore his backpack. It was a lot, when you were tired. His mom was lugging a giant flowered bag of snacks, books, passports, extra shoes, and her purse. They walked up and down long terminal halls. They made a U-turn once. It was a whole mysterious world in here.

So many cities were posted on signs at different gates—Brussels, Toronto, Rabat, Edinburgh. So many people, in such various outfits, some very modern, others looking as if they had stepped out of a history book. A man older than Sidi, with a

billowing white beard, was wearing a black top hat, carrying a loaf of bread!

Ladies wearing long dresses shimmering with bright fields of flowers smiled kindly at Aref. Some people wore shining turbans. Aref heard a crowd of teenagers speaking French. He really wished he could speak French. They were a team, dressed in striped blue and white athletic uniforms, crowding into the gate to Berlin.

Finally Aref and his mom sat down in two hard plastic chairs at the New York gate and stared at each other.

"Whew!" Aref's mother said. "We're on our way. That wasn't easy." She took a deep breath. Her forehead was damp.

"I thought Paris was supposed to be pretty," said Aref.

His mother looked surprised. “This isn’t Paris,” she said. “This is just the airport. Paris is one of the most beautiful cities in the world.”

“Really?” He looked around. Trash bins. Sandwich wrappers spilling out. “I wish we could really see Paris. Have you really seen it?”

“No. Maybe another time. Everyone loves it. The Eiffel Tower and the Louvre art museum and . . . ” Her voice trailed off.

“Why couldn’t Sidi come with us?” asked Aref. “Flying is so easy. I mean, you don’t really do *anything*. You just sit there.”

She shrugged. “I agree. It’s surely easier than driving that jeep of his.”

At the very same moment she said “jeep,” Aref heard the man wearing a black jacket

sitting across from him call out to another man, "Monsieur!" which was the name of Sidi's jeep! Maybe this meant there would be good luck for the day.

New Discoveries

Aref decided to write in his notebook until they got on the next plane. He tried to draw a picture of the airplane cockpit, which was fun and very complicated with so many buttons, dials, and lights. But already he could see he had a problem. His notebooks were usually full of things he had learned. New discoveries. And now *everything* was a discovery. He would just have to pick and choose.

Paris Stuff

1. The Paris airport is very far from the real city of Paris. You can't see anything but a gray sky and lots of trucks. It's just like a big parking lot outside.

2. Lots of people from all over the world are walking around in the Paris airport. And a man who said, "Monsieur!"

3. I heard Arabic on the moving walkway.

4. Flying was not scary. It was like sitting in any seat. I went to the cockpit and met the pilots and got wings.

5. I made more than one friend. I held one hand. That part is secret.

6. It is harder to sleep on a plane than you might think. Sitting up while sleeping feels like what Sidi called Jeep Sleep.

7. I saw a man wearing shoes that looked like small orange tiger faces with teeth on the toes.

Ocean

The Atlantic Ocean was much bigger than the Arabian Sea. It divided people. It connected them. It carried secrets and dreams. It took many hours to fly over it. You watched a cartoon with monkeys on a pirate ship. You dreamed the ocean was inside your body. You were glad you weren't a bird. You wondered if the ocean was worried about its future. You ate a cheese sandwich, then a few hours later, you ate a croissant.

New York City

At least Aref could catch a glimpse of the huge, giant, gray skyscraper city as they were landing at the airport called JFK. His hair almost stood straight up on top of his head, it looked so amazing.

"It's like Dubai!" he said.

His mom laughed. "New York was big before Dubai was big. Most of these tall buildings are older than the biggest buildings in Dubai."

Unfortunately, they didn't get to go into this city, either, just like in Paris. They didn't get to ride subways or see polar bears in Central Park or do anything fun. They only got to stand in a massive, long line which took forever to get their passports stamped.

Aref thought there might be people from one hundred different countries in the line to enter the United States. Maybe one hundred and fifty. Their musical voices and delicious accents floated on the air. He tried to eavesdrop—there were so many languages he didn't understand! He could see different-colored passports and feel shared tiredness. A little girl with messy hair was holding on to her father's leg, looking grumpy. She had a squished white rabbit in her other hand.

"We have to get our suitcases and check

them in with customs before sending them on their way again," said his mother. "Oh dear, I hope everything made it."

"Why wouldn't it?" asked Aref. He wondered what his suitcase was doing. Where was his stuffed suitcase right now?

"Sometimes suitcases get lost and go to Spain. Or Brazil," said his mother.

"Really?" Aref thought that sounded exciting, too.

He stared up to the ceiling of the huge room they were standing in and thought he saw a fluttering bird. Was he dreaming? No way! There were *two* tiny birds, swooping side by side, then landing on the rafters high above them all.

"Mom, there are birds in here!" He tugged

her hand. She looked up to where he was pointing.

"I don't see them," she said. "I'm too sleepy. My eyes won't focus."

"Look! They were flying around a minute ago, and now they are perched on that pipe, looking down on us!"

A man in a blue shirt pushing a cart with brooms, mops, and trash cans on it passed by. He looked up to where Aref was pointing. "Ah, our little friends!" he said. "You noticed them! Yes, we have birds living inside the airport."

"How do they get in?" asked Aref.

The man laughed. "The more important question is, how do they get out? Don't you think they want to get out?"

"Yes! And so do I! This line is too long! Do

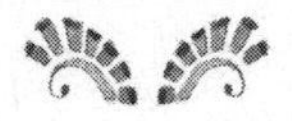

they come in through that vent?" Aref pointed to a wide, gray vent up near the ceiling.

The man laughed again. "No one can figure it out. They eat all the crumbs people drop. They come out especially at night, when the terminals are empty. One landed on my shoulder once. But they are a mystery. We can't find out how they get in, and we've been looking for a long time."

Aref thought of the huge falcon that had sat on his arm out in the desert in Oman. He had been scared it might peck him in the face. A tiny bird sitting on your shoulder would be nicer.

"Do you have any other animals in here?" he asked the man.

"Sometimes," the man replied. "We have dogs. On leashes or in small cases, traveling

with people. And the customs dogs sniffing the suitcases. And cats, in carrying boxes."

Aref wondered if he had packed anything inside his suitcase that a dog might like to sniff. He hoped so.

"Have you ever seen a fox in the airport?" he asked. "Or a turtle?"

"Ha! Never," said the man. "I'd like to see a turtle. A flying turtle! Now, that would be nice."

Spain or Brazil

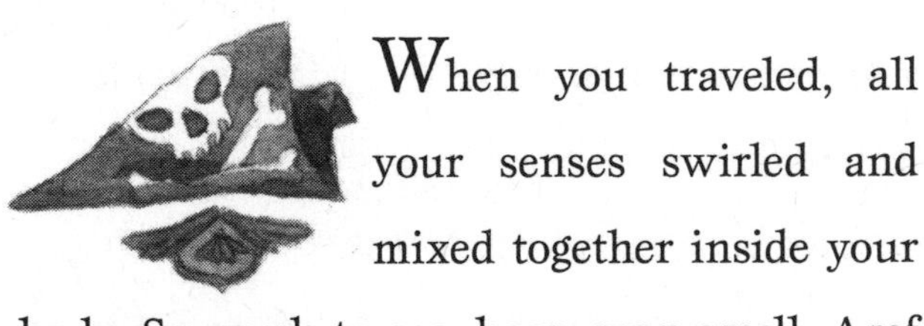

When you traveled, all your senses swirled and mixed together inside your body. So much to see, hear, even smell. Aref felt bright like a candle. Jazzed. And he wanted to remember everything.

To walk down a hall, even a boring, pale gray airport hall you had never seen before, was also interesting. What was at the end of it? Staring out the long windows, he noticed

how many trucks drove around at airports. Fuel trucks, luggage trucks, maintenance vehicles—most yellow, a few red—a whole world of trucks.

And a million people you had never seen before. Was anyone else wearing tiger shoes? Cool striped hat! Fancy watch! Worn by a man munching chips. What purple scrap of a thing did that teenager with blue hair have clutched in her hand? A tiny blue tattoo of a star marked her thumb. A very old woman wore thin, pink flip-flops like you would wear on a beach.

Aref wished he had worn his dress-up tassel around his neck to make his own self look more distinguished. But it would look strange with a T-shirt. He could have worn his stitched Omani hat, at least. He didn't see

another one like it in the crowd, though there were many turbans, scarves, baseball hats, and beanies.

How many different styles of jackets and buttons were there in the world?

How many purses? Backpacks?

How many kinds of pockets in how many different varieties and colors of pants? And what was in all those pockets? A teenager wearing what looked like a purple pirate bandanna, with skulls on it, stood right in front of them.

To be one of a huge number of people in a large space together gave Aref an oddly free feeling, as if he were invisible. Even though standing in a line this long was exhausting, his head popped with questions. Where *was* everybody going?

At least they found their suitcases! Neither suitcase had gone to Spain or Brazil. That was good luck. They rolled their bags on a big silver cart and checked them in at another desk with another conveyor belt. Airports were very organized. They had to be. Arrows and signs showed the way.

Aref hoped he might go everywhere someday.

Last Leg

"I feel so tired I could sleep for twenty hours straight," Aref's mother said as they boarded the final plane to Detroit.

"Me, too," said Aref.

Being so tired, even Aref's stomach felt confused. Was he hungry? Thirsty? It was hard to tell. Was it time for breakfast again? Who knew? The world was upside down.

Mom sighed, scrunched in her seat, and said, “At least this is the last leg.”

What did that mean, the last leg?

His mother said it meant the last part of the trip.

But why leg? Why not the last finger or last foot?

She sighed again. “Who knows? Maybe the people who invented the expression were walking.”

Then she yawned widely without even covering it, as she usually did. The captain made an announcement from the cockpit and welcomed everyone, the flight attendant gave instructions about buckling and no smoking, and they took off again. *Good-bye, New York! I barely met you! I hope to be back someday!* thought Aref.

Many of the passengers on the plane to Detroit also seemed to be coming from different countries, just as Aref and his mom were. This felt good. He wondered what they were all doing.

Two ladies wearing green-printed turbans kept smiling at him from across the aisle and nodding. A Buddhist monk in a long orange robe had paused at their row, waiting patiently for a woman with a suitcase as big as a bathtub to stuff it inside the luggage cabinet over their heads. The monk only had one small cloth purse over his shoulder. He smiled at Aref and sat down right in front of him.

This plane reminded Aref of his school back in Muscat. It felt like a parent-teacher meeting with all the different voices and languages mixing in a melodious way, nobody

fighting or feeling strange. His old school was called The American International School of Muscat, or TAISM. He loved it. He loved the way it looked, white, with bright pink flowers called bougainvillea blooming all around it. He loved the way it felt to walk proudly through its clean, wide halls filled with colorful art.

Now on the plane, he thought he heard someone speaking Danish, like some of his friends.

Soon he would be seeing his new school—Martin Luther King Jr. Elementary of Ann Arbor, Michigan—sometimes called King—for the first time. He liked how schools had nicknames. He would soon be finding his desk and meeting his new teachers. And making new friends, he hoped.

Detroit Is the City Where They Used to Make Cars

Detroit used to make more cars than any city in the world, but not now. This was one of the things Aref had discovered when he was looking up the places he would be going to.

Now China and Japan were very active in the car factory business, and Mexico, too. Aref still wanted to visit a Michigan car factory. He thought it would be interesting to see how the wheels were attached to the axles and how

they made the engine sit tightly in place, so it wouldn't fall out. He was interested in the concept of the assembly line. If you did something so many times, you became an expert. Would it be boring or fun to work on one? Riyad, one of his friends back home, wanted to design cars that looked more like little castles, with fancy rooflines and turrets on top.

Now Detroit made toffee, peanut butter, potato chips, pickles, fudge, and soda. Aref was not allowed to drink soda by either of his parents, who said it was only sugar in water and would rot your teeth out of your mouth. They said someday he would thank them. He'd had soda a few times at his friends' birthday parties, and it didn't even taste very good. His school didn't serve soda. Mostly he drank water, milk,

and lemonade with honey. And orange and apple juice, like on the plane. And tea made only with mint.

He had learned about Michigan and Detroit on the internet. Michigan was famous for blueberries and cherries. Detroit had a lot of good bakeries, he'd read, and cinnamon rolls, too. What was a cinnamon roll? Maybe he'd find out soon.

He had his yellow notebook and favorite blue Sharpie in his backpack at this moment in case something interesting popped into his mind. If you didn't write it down, you might forget it. Keeping notes and lists was still his favorite hobby. Right now he was happy it was a portable hobby.

Aref turned the pages of another airplane magazine. Men were showing their muscles,

gorgeous islands somewhere displayed happy palm trees, and women with blond hair were holding up expensive purses and smiling. From one article he learned Michigan also had the world's largest cement plant and a very big limestone quarry. He learned that people in Michigan can be called three things: Michigander, Michiganian, and Michiganite. Kids in Michigan probably had a hard time learning how to spell these things. At home in Oman, people were called Omanis. That was easier.

Sliding the magazine back into the pocket of the seat in front of him, he yawned widely and closed his eyes. Maybe he could sleep for a whole day. How long was this flight again? He was impatient to see his father. He felt a little rumpled and silly. But he had truly enjoyed

everything about their trip. He liked the tiny airplane bathrooms, like closets with clicking doors and a miniature sink. They had everything you needed, even hand lotion, which he never needed.

Greetings, Michigander!

Detroit sat on the edge of a river that connects two huge lakes and across that river was another gigantic country, Canada. Aref's father had said that maybe they could visit Canada someday. Maybe they could ride a train to get there. Far north in the province of Manitoba, fluffy polar bears were living on the ice, and the ice was melting fast, so they better get there soon.

Aref couldn't wait to see his father. It felt like a year since he had seen him, though it had only been a little more than a week. His dad had traveled ahead of them to the United States to get things ready. In that last week at home with just his mother and Sidi, Aref had had so many adventures to tell his dad about. He had gone camping with his grandfather, Sidi; slept on Sidi's flat roof; taken a boat ride on a shaky, rocking fishing boat; caught a fish and thrown it back; visited the turtle nesting beach; and held a falcon. He and Sidi had driven very far in Sidi's jeep; almost gotten lost in that mysterious, mountainous desert; and slept in a tent. He had said good-bye to everyone and packed his farewell presents. There was too much to tell.

And the biggest surprise now was that after the plane landed smoothly, and Aref and his mom walked out to Arrivals—there was Dad, standing at the bottom of the giant escalator and he *seemed to be crying*. He was holding one hand up in greeting and wearing a blue baseball cap, with two other caps in his other hand. Another blue one for Aref, and a yellow one for his mother. He plopped the caps on their heads and opened his arms wide to hug them both at once. Aref had never seen his parents cry before, except when people died. He hugged his father tightly.

"Ahlein!" his father said, hugging him back. "Welcome, welcome! You made it!"

They were blocking traffic as people streamed forward around them, pulling luggage.

"I am so happy," continued Aref's father. "My family is together now."

Aref's mother had also started crying again as she managed to spill her entire fat purse on the floor while hugging his father. She'd opened it on the escalator to turn on her telephone. Aref dove down to grab her wallet and her lipstick rolling away, and her hairbrush and tissues. What a mess!

Everyone was moving quickly toward the suitcase belts, as if there were a big race happening, but when they got to their flight's belt, it wasn't moving yet. All those giant heavy suitcases were still being unloaded from the plane.

"Sidi already sent me two emails to see if you arrived yet," Aref's dad said. "He said he was at the library taking his first

computer class and this was his homework. But he could only send emails from the library with his teacher there because, you know, he doesn't have a computer at home. Soon he will send them from his phone, I hope. We showed him how, remember? I hope he didn't forget."

"He didn't forget," Aref said. "He's very smart."

"I am just so happy to see you," said Aref's dad. He hugged Aref again. "I missed you both very much. It was such a long trip, right? It feels like a month since I saw you! I think when you travel, time stretches out. Don't you think? How did it feel, flying so far? So happy you made it!"

His dad was very talkative.

His mom was wiping her eyes, muttering

prayers under her breath. She kept holding on to his father.

"It was super fun," said Aref. "I love airplanes now!" But he was feeling anxious in a different way. This was something he had never worried about in his whole life. What do you do if both your parents start crying at once?

He changed the subject, poking at his hat. "Nice hats! Thanks, Dad."

"They are the colors of Ann Arbor," his father said. He turned the yellow one on Mom's head backward. This made her laugh.

"Do you feel like a Michigander yet?" Aref asked.

"A what? Oh yes! I really do!" said Aref's father. "That's funny. Is that what they call

it? You will like our new city a lot; it has everything."

"No," said Aref, thinking of Sidi. "It does not."

Back home, Sidi was staring at his phone. He couldn't remember one thing about sending a message from it.

Highway Signs

Dad's rental car was red. He apologized for it. "Sorry I had to get a red car," he said.

"Why are you sorry?" asked Aref. "I like it."

"They said no one else wanted it," said Aref's father. "They said people don't like red cars. Police stop you more for speeding if you are driving a red car."

That seemed strange to Aref. He climbed

into the backseat and buckled one more belt. You really had to buckle a lot of belts to get to the United States.

America! It was hard to believe! They were on the other side of the world.

He peered through the window, keeping his eye out for the police. What did American police cars even look like?

"That's okay. You're a slow driver anyway," he said to his dad. "They won't stop you."

Now that Aref thought about it, most cars were black, white, silver, or gray. He liked green cars, but you didn't see too many of those, and he really liked yellow cars, but they were even more rare.

The drive from Detroit to Ann Arbor took only forty-five minutes, but Aref had to fight to stay awake. His eyelids were drooping. He

kept drifting off. “Mom, you were wrong,” he said. “I think this is the last leg.”

She laughed. “You’re right about that!”

Green fields stretched out peacefully on both sides of the road, with nice large trees to look at, numbered exit signs, and signs for fudge. Fudge!

He shouted, “Fudge!” but his parents didn’t know what was on his list of Michigan things, so they weren’t sure why he was excited.

They passed signs for lakefront property and hotels. Restaurants that served homemade cherry pies. There wasn’t too much traffic. Aref kept his face pressed to the cool window to stay awake.

“I haven’t really seen any of the Great Lakes yet,” said his father, “but people say

they have long sand beaches like in Muscat and dunes and boats and ferries and we will love them! Michigan is the only state that touches four of them. We can go to one on a holiday someday. Michigan is really a wonderful place."

The next sign Aref saw said "Boats." He said, "Look!"

"I know I told you this before," said his father, "but there are a lot of Arabs in Michigan. There are more Arabs here, percentage-wise, than in any other American state. California and New York have a lot of Arabs, too. And they come from many different countries. I've met other graduate students from Kuwait, Palestine, Iraq, Iran, two from Oman, everywhere. We even have people from Syria and Lebanon at our

apartment complex. I think some of them might have kids."

Aref was almost asleep. He didn't want to fall asleep. He said, "That's good. Kids . . . good."

And then the signs started saying "Ann Arbor" and they were almost to their new home.

Dream While Dozing

I was eating fudge with Sidi on a boat.

He was breaking it into two pieces with his hands.

Fish were jumping out of the water.

Sidi was laughing.

I threw the fish a few chocolate crumbs.

They opened their mouths wide and caught them.

Emergency!

Dad drove slowly into town, like a tour guide, still jabbering and pointing things out. "Here is a very nice grocery store. Oasis Grill serves excellent Arabic food. . . ." but immediately after they pulled up in front of the Harmony Haven Apartments where they would live, something bad happened.

Right after they unclicked their seat belts and opened their car doors, before Aref could

even enter their new home or get a close look at a single thing yet, his mother tripped. It was a yellow parking divider she hadn't noticed. She hadn't even been walking fast, but she lost her balance and toppled face forward. Her wrist hit the pavement and snapped. Aref heard it snap.

Aref's father threw down the bags he was unloading and dashed over to help her up. She was moaning, speaking in Arabic, "Ya Allah!" Aref's father asked her in Arabic if she thought something was broken.

"Yes! Yes, I do! Broken!" She closed her eyes and kept muttering in Arabic.

A nice older couple with very pale hair dashed out of the apartment building and asked if they could do anything. "We saw you through the window!" they said. "Oh dear!"

They helped pick up Aref's mother's purse, which she had dropped again, though this time it didn't spill, and told his father about the closest hospital, which wasn't very far away.

"Do you want us to call an ambulance?" they asked.

Aref's father said that he would drive and they all helped his mother up and tucked her carefully back into the passenger side. She was moaning and shaking, but she whispered, "Thank you! Thank you!" to their new neighbors.

Aref's father put the single suitcase he had unloaded back in the trunk and slammed it shut. He drove fast, but he made some wrong turns and had to circle around. Everything felt upside down in a different way now. Aref

hadn't even seen their apartment, and now he was sitting in a green hospital waiting room, falling asleep in a chair.

It seemed so scary that bones could snap, *crack!*, in the middle of a day, when you hadn't even been doing anything exciting like waterskiing or jumping on a trampoline. What bad luck!

Aref's dad told him that the kind neighbors with the pale hair were named Mr. and Mrs. Finnegan. They had given him sugar cookies when he arrived. He had given them a box of Omani dates.

A giant clock on the wall was solemnly ticking away. Because of his extreme tiredness, Aref couldn't figure out anything about time right now. He wasn't even sure what day it was.

Two babies in strollers kept crying because their mothers were getting examined and they missed them. Another lady kept waving a stuffed orange giraffe in front of them, but only one of them liked it.

His father went back to the desk and asked if there was anything else he could do, and they said Mom would be getting an X-ray soon. *Soon* had a different meaning when you were in an emergency room.

A lady came into the waiting room and started mopping the floor . . . *swoosh, swoosh, swoosh*. The rhythm of the mop hypnotized Aref, then put him to sleep. When he opened his eyes again, the babies had disappeared.

Finally, a nurse wheeled Aref's mother into the waiting room in the wheelchair. For a

moment Aref was afraid she had broken her leg, too. But that's just what they do in hospitals, even if your legs are fine.

In three days she would have to have surgery to insert a metal plate with seven screws into her wrist. She would have to be put to sleep for a few hours with anesthesia. Now she was wearing a bulky black wrist brace, looking pained and a little scared. Aref was afraid to touch her.

"I'm sad for you, Mom," he said softly.

"Let's go home," she said. "Ya haram." Too bad. Such a shame.

What a life! You cross the wide ocean just fine on a gigantic airplane, then you trip over a curb.

Zombie Arrival

1. I felt like a real zombie by the time we got to Ann Arbor. So tired my brain was upside down. Eyes blurry. Dad said it was jet lag because we had crossed so many time zones in the air and our bodies didn't know what time it was anymore. Mom had it, too. He said we would be better in two or three days.

2. But then Mom broke her wrist, so we were sitting in a very, very cold hospital waiting room for a super-long time and I was having

dreams even while I was awake because my eyes were so blurry the elevator door looked like the mouth of a whale opening and closing.

3. It was a nice hospital. A nurse gave me a bottle of water and applesauce in a cup.

4. I was so tired I thought I was going to faint. But that would be okay because I was already at the emergency room. I took a chair nap instead.

5. Then we finally got to come to our new home. The apartment building is pretty nice. It's not as nice as our real house back in Muscat, but I didn't say that. Our apartment seems very small. We have a purple couch and striped chairs. Dad had some yellow roses in a water glass on the table. We are on the first floor. A lot of people in the world live in apartments.

6. I fell into my bed. It is a twin bed, not a wider bed like back home. I miss my real bed.

7. There is a glass tank called a terrarium (I had to ask Dad how to spell this), set up inside my bedroom on a table, with a purple stone inside and a little plastic palm tree and a dish for water. I said, "Dad! What is this?" He said, "We will find you a turtle."

8. Look how much I wrote, and we haven't even done anything yet.

9. I slept for the next 100 hours.

The American Way

That night, or maybe it was the next, the Finnegans from next door brought over a steaming pot of tomato vegetable soup, hot biscuits with a plate of butter, and folded-over apple pies, like half-moons, that they had baked in their oven. Everything smelled so good.

Mrs. Finnegan said the pies were called "hand pies" because a person could hold one in one hand.

"Perfect for my mom then," Aref said.

"Well, enjoy!" said Mrs. Finnegan.

"This is very nice of you," said Aref's father.

"This is the American way," said Mr. Finnegan. "You had a hard start; things will get better now."

Aref's mother was all crumpled on the end of the couch looking like a mouse, but she sat up straight and tried to smile. "Really, you are the kindest," she said.

Mrs. Finnegan patted Aref on the shoulder. She said to him, "I could tell how proud of you your father is, because of the way he talks about you."

The way he talks about you. Somehow Aref had never imagined his father talking about him to other people. It made him feel like standing up straight.

After the Finnegans left, Aref and his parents sat around the table for the first time as a family in their new world. The soup tasted yummy and healthy. Tomato broth, green beans, fresh corn, barley . . . the biscuits were puffy and perfect.

As for the hand pies, Aref ate one, then another.

They were delicious.

Hospital Clock

Aref talked to Sidi, and Sidi sounded far away, crackly.

Sidi said, "Everything misses you!"

Sidi said, "I saw Diram at the grocery store. He asked about you!"

Diram was Aref's best friend back home. They played on the school soccer team together. They had never had a fight, not even one.

But after Aref talked to Sidi, he felt worse

rather than better. He did not know how he could survive three years without his grandfather's gentle voice at his side. He went to his room and lay on his bed and stared up at the ceiling. It was light gray.

Early the next morning, Aref sat at the small kitchen table in the dark, eating a bowl of Raisin Bran with bananas before they took his mother to the hospital. She wasn't allowed to eat anything before the surgery. Aref's father said he would find something to eat at the hospital, then stuck a banana into his jacket pocket. He grabbed two oat granola bars and stuck those in, too.

From the backseat of the car, Aref noticed the skinny moon still in the sky. Inside his head he said, "Hi, moon. We really need you now."

At the hospital Aref and his father sat in a special waiting room. Some old people, older than Sidi, were quiet and hunched together in the corner. A younger man was reading a magazine. There were no babies today. Too bad!

On the wall a giant clock was telling the wrong time, its hands stuck in place. Aref didn't wear a watch, but he knew it was wrong. It had barely gotten light outside. He asked his father if they could fix it, but he said, "No, son, it's not our clock."

The friendly nurse at the desk heard them talking and said, "We tried to get that old thing repaired, but we need a whole new clock." She was wearing glasses with bright red frames. She shook her head and said, "Things can be very slow around here sometimes."

"Do you have any different clocks, maybe

in a closet or something?" Aref was feeling nervous about his mom, so he just kept jabbering. "My dad could climb a ladder and put one up for you."

Aref's father touched his arm to quiet him down.

"Helpful boy!" the nurse said. "Let me make a call right now and see if maintenance can find us one. That clock has been stuck at noon for a really long time. I'll tell them we have a special request."

Maintenance turned out to be a guy with a lot of little braids and a hammer in his pocket. His pants and shirt were the same color blue. He waved a large square box at them and said, "To the rescue! No one should be timeless in a waiting room!" He got a ladder and placed it under the clock. He pulled a new clock out

of a box. Aref asked if he needed him to help hold the ladder steady.

"No, I'm fine." The man stared at Aref a minute, then said, "You know what? I like you." Then he said, "Where you from, son?"

Aref wondered how the man knew he was from somewhere else. His voice? His shoes? "Oman," he said.

"Oh man? Where is that?" asked the man.

Aref looked at his father. How did you describe it?

"Oman is on the other side of the world, next to Saudi Arabia, but much smaller," Aref said. "It is a very nice country with mountains and long beaches and deserts and giant turtle nesting grounds."

"Really? Frankly, I never heard of it," said the man. "You've actually been there?"

"I grew up there! We both did!" Aref pointed at his father. "I just got here three days ago. Straight from there."

"And you're already at the hospital?" asked the man. "I wish you better luck!"

"It's my mom who had bad luck," said Aref.

But now at least they knew what time it was. And the man knew where Oman was. It was 8:45 a.m. At 10:10 the doctor returned and said that Aref's mother had "done great" and would be in recovery for about thirty minutes. Aref's father held both of the doctor's hands while thanking him.

Finally, at 10:45, a nurse pushed Aref's mother into the waiting room. She stood up from her wheelchair smiling weakly and holding up her wrapped hand that now looked like a paw. The worst part was over.

Chore Dog

Because of his mother's injury, Aref had twice as many chores to do.

"I like doing chores," he told the Finnegans when they came by to see how surgery had gone.

They were impressed that he was unpacking his mother's clothes from her suitcase and hanging them in her closet.

Making beds had never been his favorite

activity, but his mother said, "It's hard to make a bed with one hand; please help me, my love." So he stood on the other side of the bed and helped her smooth the sheets. Then he said, "I'm an expert!" and made the beds all by himself. He said what she usually said after everything was neat again, "Ahhhh, victory!"

His father did the laundry in the washer and dryer tucked in a closet in the kitchen. They both folded the clothes and towels.

Aref swept and mopped and vacuumed. Just like back home in Oman, the dustpan was his friend. He used a tall white brush to scrub the toilet, then stood the brush back up in its little brush house. His father taught him how to load the dishwasher, add the soap, and turn it on when it got full. At night they read books

and watched movies. They played dominoes and cards on the kitchen table. Aref's father didn't want to explore much yet. He said they needed to stay home and take care of Mom.

One day Aref wrapped his mother's old orange scarf around his head, making a turban, because his mom always used to do this herself when she did chores. He stared into the mirror and frowned. He pinched his lips together to look like Ummi Salwa, their ancient one-hundred-year-old neighbor back home.

And that was only part of it.

Aref wrote the grocery list. He would stand next to his mom, who was resting on the couch, and say, "What else, Mom? Anything else?" Sometimes he drew pictures on the list—a smiling apple, an angry-looking carton of eggs. He drew a tipsy hat on a bunch of

bananas and put giant ears on the watermelon. At the grocery store, he helped his father find what they needed and loaded the cart. He loved the grocery store in Ann Arbor as much as he had loved the LuLu Hypermarket back home. So many kinds of cheese! Mountains of different lettuces! He was glad to see pita bread on a special rack near the loaves of American bread. He was surprised the nuts were in bags and jars instead of giant barrels with sacks and scoops.

Aref helped his dad carry the grocery bags inside the apartment and unload them. Back in Oman, his father had usually been at work all day and didn't come home until it was time for dinner. In fact, Aref had hardly ever seen him unpack groceries, *ever.*

Now, they lined up the groceries on the

counter, and put them away. Everything had a place.

They were making new places.

In the apartment kitchen, Aref helped his dad chop things, mix salads, squeeze lemons, shake salt. He stirred pots of lentil soup on the stove, while standing on a small stool. His father was trying to learn how to cook and Aref helped him, mixing batter for pancakes, peeling carrots. His father was surprised at all the things Aref knew how to do.

Thank goodness there was a pizza restaurant on the corner of their street. People in Oman liked pizza, too, including Aref, and he was happy that the pizza place in Ann Arbor was so close to their apartment. They went there a lot. They lined up at the counter to get their pizza pie in a flat white box that was hot. A

little farther away was the Oasis Grill, serving stuffed grape leaves and hummus and tabouleh and bread baked fresh every day, and double thank goodness for that. There was even a fish restaurant near the university campus where they ordered crispy fish sandwiches like they used to eat in Muscat, and french fries. It could still taste like home even far away.

Aref noticed that his father often seemed worried about everything, which was strange, because he used to act more relaxed. He started saying, "Ya haram!" a lot, which meant, "Oh dear! What a shame!" In Muscat, his dad used to sing in the shower and joke all the time, and leave surprises around the house, just like Sidi did.

"It is hard to get into new routines," Aref's father said. "But I'm working on it."

Sometimes they heard sirens, and Aref wished they could go follow them and see what was happening.

A big pile of school papers, forms, bills, and newspapers started piling up on the table. Some of the envelopes hadn't even been opened. Aref's father tended closely to his mother, waiting on her, changing the TV channel, bringing her ice water and hot tea. She never used to watch TV, but now she was sitting around a lot, staring at cooking shows or looking out the window. For Aref, it was the first time he had seen one of his parents suffer. It was hard.

"You're lucky," his father said to him softly. "Many people suffer. She'll be better soon."

Aref's turtle terrarium was still empty, but he didn't say anything.

My News

1. Dad took me to a place called the Wave Field. It is a big field with baby mountains of grass. No one else was there. I could run up and down the baby mountains. We went after dinner, but before sunset, because the light is good then. I pretended they were regular-size mountains and I was a giant.

2. Also we went to a farmers market to buy super-fresh lettuce and little cucumbers and pink flowers called zinnias. It was like the souk

back home because it was all outside. People were nice and giving tastes. Dad tried some homemade cheese with chives in it. A farmer gave me a small cup of ice cream. He told me I could visit his cows. I asked if I could milk one and he said a machine milks them, but I could watch. We took Mom a surprise hamburger (huge) from a place called Krazy Jim's Blimpy Burger.

3. We passed Fleetwood Diner with a line of people waiting outside it. Dad said it had good salads. We didn't go there because we already had lettuce.

Isn't it strange to wait in line for a salad?

Low Notes

At first Aref thought it was fun to go with his parents to the University of Michigan campus. Many buildings were made of bricks, with arches over the upstairs windows and little statues or faces on the corners at the top. Aref could walk on the low garden walls, jump off, and run on the smooth concrete pathways.

Parts of the campus seemed more like

a park than a school. The Wave Field was already his favorite spot. It was incredible that Michigan hosted more than one hundred different species of trees. Aref liked to smell their bark and leaves. He was a sniffing detective. His father said he had the best nose in the family.

It was funny to see one's own parents being students again. At home in Muscat, Aref's parents were the professors standing in the front of their classrooms full of students. The very first time Aref's parents met, at Muscat University, they told each other that studying was their favorite activity in the whole world. Seriously!

You could go from being a teacher to being a student again very quickly.

"Students are lucky!" his mother said.

"Sitting in class is relaxing. I don't have to give the whole lesson, and I like soaking up new information."

Aref would carry his own book or drawing pad and colored pencils and markers in his backpack, sit at a desk in the back corner of the classroom, scribble, doodle, and enter his own world. He would take new books he had checked out of the library. Right now he was reading about bats. Fruit bats had excellent eyesight. They used "echolocation"—the reflection of sound waves—to help them hunt for insects. He knew there were around fourteen different species of bats in Oman, but was shocked to learn there are about 1,330 different species in the whole world. So many! They are the only mammal really able to fly, which should give them truly high

status among all creatures, and it was too bad that so many people were scared of bats, because they were not something to be scared of. Aref admired them.

Sometimes Aref went to his father's biology classes and sometimes he went to his mom's English classes. He thought it might have been more interesting if his parents were studying to be medical doctors instead of just college professor doctors. Then he could have watched operations and surgeries, like the one on his mom's wrist. He would not want to see any babies being delivered, however.

"Good morning!"

"Good morning!"

It was amazing how quickly routines were born. His mom already had friends in class who helped her unpack her notebook and tiny

tape recorder which she used to record the lecture since her hand was still swollen and purple and looked like an eggplant. She could also record on her phone, but didn't want to fill it all up.

At first Aref carried a small bag of popcorn or chips or an apple for a snack during class, but his mother said he made loud crunchy sounds and told him he couldn't bring a noisy food. He could bring cheese or a muffin. He asked his dad to buy him a phone so that he could listen to music or play games, but his dad said no. His dad said, "That will get in the way of your own thoughts." But Aref was ready for something to get in the way of his thoughts!

After a few weeks of this tag-along life, Aref was wishing his own school started sooner.

He stared at people who knew each other walking down halls and sidewalks together. Would he find new friends and walk with other people soon? Would he belong? Would he still feel like himself? Or would he keep feeling a little lost, like those birds in the airport terminal? He was wishing Sidi were here to have exciting adventures with him. He was even wishing for a babysitter!

Where We Are Now

The city of Ann Arbor didn't seem as new as Aref had imagined it would. It seemed even nicer than new, rooted in place, many buildings a little old and faded, in a pleasant way. Some whole entire blocks had buildings constructed of red bricks. In Oman, the very ancient Bahla Fort, magical as a castle, way out in the desert, was constructed of brownish gray bricks on huge stone foundations. Aref

had loved visiting it with Sidi. But he had not seen red bricks before, and he liked to think about building with bricks when he was going to sleep. What a lot of work it would be, stacking all those bricks, spreading mortar between! Some buildings in Ann Arbor had green awnings over their windows and doors, which looked friendly. Also, the giant trees growing on almost every block were very appealing. They sat in little squares of dirt inside the sidewalks.

There were no palm trees at all.

Aref's father, being a biologist, would fill his pockets with seeds and leaves as they walked, things to study later. He bought some red and yellow pots at the dollar store and a few sacks of soil. He said they would make a garden for Mom on their patio. He bought

Aref's mother a red geranium, which she loved, and a small trowel and shovel for Aref to use. The tools had red and green handles, but felt heavy and professional. Aref got to fill the pots. They would sing some old folk songs in Arabic while they dug. His dad used to sing these to him when he was a baby.

Aref's father told Aref that Michigan had around fourteen billion trees in total. It was impossible to comprehend numbers like that!

"We are living in a forest," Aref's father said. "That's very exciting for people who grew up in a desert country."

Aref liked the names of some of the trees very much. His favorites were sugar maple, black cherry, quaking aspen, and bigtooth aspen. In the breezes, their leaves sounded

like rustling lullabies, another soft tune he tried to hum. Those leaves were whispering deep secrets. They made him feel far back in time and a little lonely.

Tree Questions

1. Does a quaking aspen worry about earthquakes?

2. Does a bigtooth aspen have a bird for a dentist? I read that this aspen can get very old. Does it ever need false teeth?

Dreamkeepers

One afternoon Aref and his father drove over to Martin Luther King Jr. Elementary School to fill out some papers for his own enrollment. A poster outside the office proclaimed, "The King Dreamkeepers—Keeping the Dream Alive Every Day!" The school was fifty years old, older than his school back home, older than his mom and dad.

The atmosphere felt warm from the

minute you walked in. There was a lot to look at. Posters! Artwork! The polished bathrooms! The hallways had names on actual metal street signs: *Kindness Road* and *Dignity Avenue.*

On the main office wall a bright poster announced, "Arts Camp." The camp was starting in a week, right here at school, for students in grades three to five. Aref tugged on his dad's arm. "Maybe I could go to that?"

Aref did not feel that he was a very good artist, not as good as some of his friends back home, but he had heard all the university lectures he could stand. He was not ready to be in college.

Maybe he could make some friends if he went to a camp? He had been in Ann Arbor

a few weeks already and had not talked to a single kid.

Without even discussing it with his mom, his dad signed him up. Aref felt excited. Something was happening! What would he need to bring? The lady behind the desk said, "Just come on Monday—your teacher will have all the supplies. Welcome!"

Wow!

When they stepped back onto the side-walk, Aref said, "Thanks, Dad! The music in my head has changed."

"What do you mean?" asked his father.

"For a while I was only hearing the low notes," replied Aref.

Dear Sidi,

How are you? I get to write email now, to talk to you!

I hope you will answer right away.

How is Monsieur?

We have a rented red car, not a jeep. I am going to go to arts camp. We already talked about what happened to Mom. It wasn't good. I heard the snap. She still can't write.

I miss you. FLYING WAS NOT HARD! You could do it.

Will you please please do it?

And also I have a secret I will tell you right now. I am going to get my own turtle! Someday soon we are going to go to a pet store and pick one out. The turtle's house is already in my room. It will not be a sea turtle ha ha, he would fill the

whole room. My room is small. It's okay.

Have you seen Mish-Mish?

I miss you so much. I want to talk to you next time Mom and Dad call you. Sorry I was asleep the last time.

The U.S. does not feel too strange. We have more trees here. I will learn their names and make a list for you. Here is the start of the list—

red pine

white pine

bigtooth aspen

Trees don't have teeth! But the bigtooth can live to be older than you are. Come see it!

Love, Aref

My Favorite Color Is Every Color

1. On the first day of arts camp, the teacher, Ms. Liddy, asked us what our favorite color was. Then she told us to make a picture of our favorite place with our favorite color. But I had a problem. My favorite color is every color. So I made a regular picture with many colors. She didn't get mad. I drew the beach in Muscat and some of the buildings and the mountains behind them. I put a lot of different colors

on the heads of people walking on the beach. Turbans and scarves. It looked like a rainbow. She liked it.

2. My new friends are Malek, Robin, Jamie, and Frankee. He said he spells it with two e's, but most people don't. He likes to be different. His real name is Francis, but he hates it. He was wearing two different-colored socks, one red and one white. He laughs a lot.

3. The girls are Jameela, Lucy, and Annie. Jameela came from Afghanistan. She lived through a lot of fighting in her country. She asked me if there was fighting in Oman, and I said never. Sultan Qaboos does not like fighting. Oman is a peaceful country. She said I was lucky.

4. We have fun and I don't feel strange at

all. Malek is shy. Every person is a different color anyway—different hair, different skin, but good together, just like my drawing. Also, just like at home.

Grape Arbor

"Everyone seems shocked that I speak such good English," said Aref. "That is not what I was worried about."

He was sitting at the kitchen table after arts camp, swinging his legs, eating his usual snack of bananas, peanut butter, and crackers. A beam of sunlight lit up the glass saltshaker in the middle of the table, just the way it used to in Muscat.

"What are your worries?" asked his mother. She was sitting on their patio studying. She liked to keep the door open to their little hideaway. They all did. It was their private outdoor place. Aref mumbled something. He knew it annoyed her when he mumbled. Sometimes he did it on purpose.

"What is that, habibi? What did you say?"

He could hear the edge in her voice.

"I said, do we have any more bananas?"

He could have said, "You broke your wrist and can't do anything and Dad isn't the same, either. Also, I miss my best friend in the whole world, my Sidi, and he didn't even answer my email yet!"

Aref had told the kids at arts camp that all the kids at his school in Muscat spoke English.

They were surprised. They said, "Really? Why?" *He* was surprised by things that surprised other people.

"Because it is an international school," he said. "So we have to speak one language that many people know."

"We are living in an international world," said Ms. Liddy.

After Aref wrote the name of his home country on the blackboard in Ms. Liddy's classroom, Frankee said, "Oh man! You come from Oh man? Is that really a place?"

Not that again.

"It is a really great place," said Aref proudly. "But Michigan is nice, too."

"Is it full of cats?" asked Lucy.

Why did she say that? He hadn't mentioned his cat Mish-Mish to anyone.

"Because Muscat has 'cat' in it," continued Lucy.

Aref had never thought of that.

"Do you know what the nickname of Ann Arbor is?" asked a kid Aref hadn't met yet.

"No!" said Aref.

"A squared!" shouted almost everyone at the same time.

"I like A-two better," said Annie. "We say A-two in my family."

"Who was Ann?" Aref asked.

"Ann?" said Frankee.

"Ann Arbor," said Aref. "Was she a real girl or a lady?"

Annie was smiling while they discussed this.

None of the kids knew the answer, but Ms. Liddy did.

"It turns out," said Ms. Liddy, "that there were two founders of the town, long ago, and their wives were named Ann and Ana. These people planted a grape arbor, and everyone liked to sit in its green leafy shade when evening came. So they decided to call their nice shady place 'Ann's Arbor,' and over the years the *s* got dropped."

There was always a story.

My Worries in A2

1. Sidi doesn't write every day like he said he would. In fact, he has not written me once.

2. We have not heard any news at all about Mish-Mish. Has she run away already?

3. Have my cousins written on the walls of my room back home with my crayons? I hope not!

4. Will I be able to draw a better face when I finish arts camp? My faces look like bobbleheads. Ms. Liddy is so nice to us. She says, "Just do your best."

5. If I put a turtle in my terrarium, will it knock to get out? Will it feel trapped? A spiny softshell turtle looks like a gray pancake and has a nose like a pig snout. I want to see one! Ms. Liddy likes that I draw a turtle under my name.

Lonely Moon

The night sky looked tipped here. Stars floated in different places. The moon wore an altered gaze. There was mist in the air. Places with lakes and rivers had lots of mist. Also, when they went to the desert together, Sidi had said the moon would be an old friend always, looking calmly down on Aref, carrying Sidi's thoughts to him wherever Aref went. It would be their link. But Sidi may

have been wrong about this.

Sometimes the moon over Michigan looked like a different moon, farther away, shrouded with a foggy scarf. And Aref couldn't hear Sidi's thoughts very well at all.

Aref remembered the quiet breath of the desert back home. It was always there. Even in the city, you could stand outside and it would soak into you instantly. It lay patiently on the edge of town. When he and Sidi stood together staring up at the moon, their feet sank down a little, desert gravity.

You could not feel that desert breathing on you from this far away.

Mixed-Up Dreams

For the first time in his life, Aref had dreams at night in which he was two people. The two Arefs were dressed the same, like in a mirror. They were conversing with each other. That's how he knew there were two.

"They are mispronouncing my name," one Aref said. "They are saying 'Air-if.'"

Actually, his name was pronounced

R-F—like the letters, with a little roll of the tongue—which should be easy, right?

The second Aref said, "You need to correct them. How can they know if you don't correct them?"

"But that might make them mad," said the first Aref.

Then they talked about zinnias and cow-milking machines.

At breakfast Aref asked his dad, "What should I do if my new friends say my name wrong?"

"Say, 'Hey! I'm so happy to be friends with you,'" his father replied. "'But really my name is pronounced R-F. Just like the two letters!' Then you could ask, 'Am I saying *your* name right?'"

“Really?” Aref said.

“Why not? It’s not a big deal. They would want to say it right.”

Aref was starting to ache. He really, *really* wanted to go hiking and get lost in a giant forest. He wanted to wander with his dad alone, because his mom might fall in a hole and break the other wrist. Michigan seemed like a perfect place to get lost in a forest. He wanted to explore! What would it feel like to be swallowed by a crowd of trees? He imagined their whispering. This was not something he could do back home in Oman. In Oman there were palm trees and a few oases. There were sinkholes and springs and strings of elegant camels striding across the tops of shifting sand dunes.

But in Michigan there were more trees than people.

Aref wished he could at least ride a bike around the parking lot. But he didn't have a bike here. His bike was so far away. One night in his dreams, he was riding his bike around the parking lot at the LuLu Hypermarket back home. What a strange dream! He had never done that in real life. There were too many cars.

Sometimes when his mother took a nap, Aref went to see if Mrs. Finnegan was looking out her window. She would wave him in to have a little cookie and talk to her. He'd leave a note for his mother and lock the door behind him when he visited next door. He had his own key on a green turtle key ring. Mrs. Finnegan showed him pictures

of Ireland, where she had come from a long time ago, and where she still had cousins. She told him about the snowmobiles and skating and sledding and cross-country skiing in Michigan. Aref couldn't wait to see snow. He thought snow falling from the sky, coating all the buildings and streets with white icing, would be the most exciting thing he had ever seen.

The kids at arts camp said snow was the best when it first fell down, but then it got sloppy. It looked like whipped cream and mashed potatoes in the beginning, then quickly started looking like mud.

No one could believe he had never seen snow.

"That's impossible!" Robin said. "Everybody sees snow!"

"No, they don't," said Aref. "Probably millions of people in the world have never seen snow!"

"A lot of kids in the United States have never even seen snow," said Ms. Liddy. "Like in Florida, Arizona . . . "

"I've never seen an ocean," said Robin, shrugging. "I only see big lakes."

No one but Aref had ever seen a sea turtle crawling up onto a beach, from the waves. No one had ridden a camel. No one had held a falcon.

Aref wanted boots. He wanted to visit a dairy farm and milk a cow.

More Things People Might Not Have Seen

1. The sultan's yacht
2. A machine slicing potatoes and another machine making potato chips (I want to see this)
3. A baby turtle hatching out of an egg on a beach filled with turtle nests
4. A spider spinning its web while you sleep
5. Your heart beating inside your own body

New Stuff

1. I haven't seen one single turtle since I got here, even though I still have my "Turtles in Michigan" folder. I pinned it to my wall over the terrarium. The wood turtle looks like it's been carved from wood. The eastern box turtle can close its shell all the way, like a real box. I'm ready to go to the pet store! Mr. Finnegan said we could also see some in the woods, or visit a lake or a pond. But I can't go by myself. And could I really take a turtle

away from a lake to live in a room? Wouldn't that be mean? What about his family? What if it was a girl and her eggs had just hatched?

2. The yogurt in small cups here is not as good as Sidi's yogurt in the big bowl. I miss that taste. His is sour, in a good way.

3. Eggs live in every country.

4. At arts camp we are making collages with old magazines, cutting them up, and also using markers and paint and stickers and newspapers and glitter, making self-portraits. On my face I pasted a little turtle for one eye and an airplane for the other.

5. Next we will do printmaking, which looks really fun.

6. Mom likes barbeque.

Away on Vacation

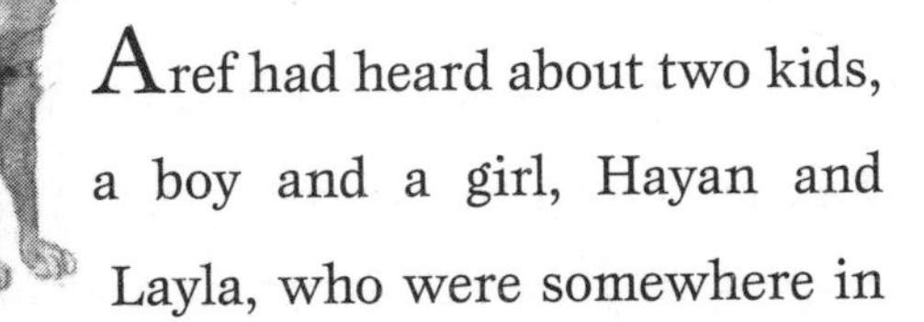

Aref had heard about two kids, a boy and a girl, Hayan and Layla, who were somewhere in the Middle East visiting their grandparents. They lived in the apartment building next to his. They were a little older than he was. But everyone said they were funny and nice. And they spoke Arabic, too, and had bicycles. Such luck!

And he'd heard about the man right

next door named Hugh, who couldn't see and lived with his golden retriever helper dog named Honeybun. Hugh had gone to Arizona to visit his sister who also couldn't see, and ran a lumberyard. He stayed with her every summer because he said he really loved the heat. Even before meeting Hugh, Aref thought he might like Oman, where sometimes it got up to 122 or 130 degrees Fahrenheit in the summer. This was partly why all the men wore white, because it kept you cooler.

Mrs. Finnegan said, "Hayan and Layla are funny. They're a little shy. You're not shy. They laugh a lot. They'll like you. And you will be surprised how much Hugh can do for himself. He doesn't really need any help. People don't know enough about blind people,

and they should learn more. Of course, Hugh has Honeybun if he gets in a jam."

Aref wanted to meet Hugh because their living room wall was the other side of Hugh's living room wall. This was something interesting about apartments. Maybe they could knock on the wall at night and send messages in Morse code.

Aref wondered if they would all be friends. And he really wanted to meet Honeybun, because the Finnegans said that Honeybun was so smart, he could answer Hugh's commands as if he spoke English. Sometimes, when Honeybun was very happy or needed to go outside, he also hummed. Probably he could make a phone call if he needed to.

In the early evenings, Aref and his parents

often went out walking in the soft light. Once they stopped at the Italian restaurant on the corner and ate spaghetti and meatballs. There were chunks of delicious garlic bread steaming in a basket on the table, and the three of them ate it all up and requested more. A juggler on the sidewalk was juggling three red balls. People stopped to watch him. They threw coins into a hat. The juggler could even juggle behind his back.

Many shops and restaurants had cheerful notices posted on the doors that said, "Happy summer!" then mentioned their owners were "away on vacation." Ann Arbor was much smaller in summers because so many students went away.

"Where do they all go?" Aref asked the Finnegans.

"They go back to their homes in other places to see their families, or they study somewhere else, or become an intern, or they get jobs in different cities or countries, or maybe they go traveling with backpacks and sleeping bags."

Sleeping bags! Aref wanted a sleeping bag. He wanted it to be blue with small green turtles lined up on it, like one he'd seen in a picture book one time.

How much he wished he could still be camping out with Sidi! They had unrolled their beautiful cotton blankets from the Night of a Thousand Stars camp in the desert and slept like babies in tents under the sky's great canopy.

Now Aref held his father's hand when he walked, which he hadn't done for a long time.

That was a baby thing. But it just seemed right here, in this country, as they were finding their way.

Aref liked the crosswalk signals in Michigan a lot, the walking man and the red hand. These signs had started coming to Oman, too, but there were more of them here. In Ann Arbor they also talked. "Wait! Wait!" boomed the big voice from the pole. The flat silver buttons seemed hopeful, ready to be pressed. Aref liked pushing them with his elbow.

Once they saw Frankee walking with his own dad downtown, and Frankee called out, "Yo man from O-man!"

Aref and his father had laughed.

Now when they walked back from anywhere, shopping or camp or eating, their

apartment complex seemed to welcome them home.

Home happened fast.

They recognized their building from a distance and headed straight past all other doors toward their own red door. They waved at people they didn't know yet. Already they knew the fluffy pink bushes near their front step.

The oranges were sitting in a wooden bowl in the center of their kitchen table.

Everything already felt familiar.

Not Fine

Back home, Sidi was having some troubles he wasn't telling them about. He didn't want to go anywhere he and Aref had ever gone together, because then he missed Aref too much.

This was a problem.

They had gone everywhere.

Sidi tried shopping at a different grocery market, where he had never taken Aref, but it was hard to find his favorite foods. It took

him thirty minutes to find olives. He needed a map inside the store and went home feeling exhausted.

Sidi tried walking on a different beach to watch the lovely sky cool down, but the tipsy fishing boats and patient waves and happy children calling out, running, playing with balloons and beach balls, made him feel lonely.

Sidi used to joke about being an astronaut, but now he really felt like one, lost in space.

He even stopped making yogurt, because Aref had loved it so much. The blue bowl and wooden spoon gave Sidi sad feelings.

Also, he had trouble sleeping, which had never happened before in his whole life.

Well, maybe twice . . . when he was a little boy and had a nightmare about a twisty octopus rising up out of the sea to grab him, or

when he and Aref slept together on the hard roof and his back ached.

Now he lay awake until midnight, staring at the ceiling, fingering his prayer beads, sighing. He rolled from side to side, then woke again at three a.m. with a tummy ache.

But he didn't tell Aref this in his emails, which he finally started pounding out slowly and carefully during his computer classes at the library. He wrote instead, "Today I ate five peanuts—and two oranges. Plus a few other things. There was a bad traffic jam by the souk. But I am fine."

August

Heat, and ice cream, and jumping in the swimming pool at the apartments!

Finally the neighbors had returned!

Hayan knew how to dive from the side of the pool, gracefully, like a real Olympic diver. They didn't have a diving board at the apartment pool, but he said he could dive from the high one at the park. Aref and Layla just watched him with wonder. When Aref

tried to dive, water went up his nose. Layla wouldn't even try. She stood at the side of the pool, holding a pink mouse with a long green ribbon tail. Aref noticed that she carried it everywhere.

Sometimes Hayan brought a blue plastic ball to the pool, and a floating net, or twisty green worms as big as pillows to float on. They brought juice in plastic cups. You couldn't have glass by the pool.

By August, Aref's parents were taking exams for their summer courses. It seemed strange that adults had to take tests when they went to school, too. Every evening while they were studying or writing papers or doing research, Aref sat at the kitchen table, sketching turtles with his colored pencils and painting watery scenery with

watercolors. He was getting better by the minute! He could feel it. Ms. Liddy had taught them to "use their mistakes." She said there were no mistakes. He really liked painting waves, letting the blues blend on the page. Sometimes he blew on the wet paint to make it move.

One day the entire arts camp marched together to visit the University of Michigan Museum of Art. They took notes on their favorite paintings or sculptures, and then later that day made a piece inspired by something they saw.

That was the first time Aref painted nonstop in watercolors. He had fallen in love with a painting by an artist named Paul Klee that reminded him of Oman. The tag on the painting said Paul Klee's nickname had been

"the little Arab," though he wasn't an Arab. He lived in Switzerland.

Aref made a sky with a small pale green island floating in it. That island had puffy edges like a cloud, and one boy sitting on it, his arms raised.

Aref's father took Aref downtown to buy him some beautiful Japanese colored pencils and his own big watercolor box and three soft brushes of different sizes. Also a fat pad of watercolor paper.

Making art seemed more fun than studying for exams. Aref could tell this was true by staring at his parents' faces in the evening light.

The best part of arts camp for Aref was something he loved back home, too. Clay.

"It's like playing in the mud!" Frankee said.

Ms. Liddy laughed. "It *is* mud," she said.

Annie said she didn't like her fingers all sticky. But Aref loved smoothing and shaping the damp clay with his fingertips. He liked breaking it into cool chunks. He liked making small animals with large heads and rounded paperweights and a plate with a fish etched into its face. Jameela made a round shape with a poked-in-place that she said was an outdoor bread oven in Afghanistan. They even got to mix their own glazes from iron oxide dust, pouring water out of little cups, then stirring it. Aref had never done that before. It was like mixing a recipe.

Painting the pots with brushes and glaze before they fired them was exciting. You

could make stripes or polka dots. Aref stuck his finger into the side of a vase and gave it a face. He made it look like Sidi and wasn't even sure how he did that. The tilt of the smile? The eyebrows?

He would give it to his mother as a present when it was done. He would put a flower in it. They fired their pots in a kiln. Some kids wanted to blacken their pots in a barbeque pit outdoors to make them look ancient. Aref did not. But afterward the "ancient" pots looked so good, he wished he had.

And then, toward the very end of camp, they had some extra clay fun. They got to fire their coasters and bowls and vases in a hole in the ground. This was the old way, and it took three days. Only Ms. Liddy and their classroom assistant, Coco, could light the fires.

Aref and all his camp friends walked to a gravel pit in a vacant lot next door to their school and helped dig a big hole in the dirt, for burying their pots. Ms. Liddy and Coco lit the fire with crumpled-up papers, just like a campfire, which ignited the sticks, then the coals. The slow-burning fire couldn't catch anything else on fire because gravel didn't burn.

It was strange shoveling gravel back over the buried fire and pots.

Three days later they walked back and dug their pots out very carefully. The pots and plates and cups and little animals were now cooked. Solid, hard, like real pots. Some were reddish with iron oxide, some were more brown, some were white.

Jameela cried because her oven-shaped paperweight had exploded. She said, "My

things always explode." Aref didn't know what this meant. Nothing of hers had exploded during arts camp. They had to let her cry for a while.

Then they had to let their pots cool in the field.

They ran around flying kites they had folded and glued from Japanese papers. Some of the kites flew better than others. Lucy fell and said she sprained her ankle. They had snacks—juice boxes and Chex mix and carrots and cookies.

Then they picked up their pots and walked back to school. Ms. Liddy surprised them with a big cake that said, "We Are All Artists!" in blue icing across white frosting. And they ate it and hugged.

"See you in school!" everyone said.

✱ ✱ ✱

Walking home with Dad, Aref realized something he hadn't really thought about before.

A light came on in his head.

When school started, he would already have friends.

New Things

1. I learned A2 is also called Tree Town. How can one town have so many nicknames?

2. Mom doesn't like when I say "A-squared" or "A2." She says it sounds like another planet. She likes the word arbor.

3. Sidi told me it rained so much back home, the waterfalls in Salalah were "roaring." I wish I could hear that.

4. Rock climbers from England and Europe

visited Oman and did an expedition up some of the steepest cliffs and saw some of the very special Arabian leopards!!!!! We saw this on TV. A scientist of Oman has been videotaping them in the wild. There was a girl and a boy leopard slinking around the rocks. There are only around 200 left alive. Very, very rare. Sidi and I always joked about wanting to run into them.

5. I think there are no leopards in Michigan. Except maybe at a zoo.

Hugh Comes Home

After reading awhile, and eating a cheesc and tomato sandwich as a snack, Aref heard some clinking and clanking and opened the front door to see if Robin, his friend from school who was coming for a sleepover, had arrived yet.

No Robin. But there was a fluffy golden dog standing between the bushes and the parking lot. The dog was scanning the parking lot, as if waiting for a ride, and turned his

head slowly to look at Aref. His eyes looked steady and kind.

Aref walked toward him and said, "Are you Honeybun? Did Hugh get home?"

The dog looked as if he wanted to talk. Would he hum? Aref thought so!

Just then the door of the next apartment opened and a tall man wearing jeans, a red plaid shirt, and a blue denim jacket stepped out. He was holding a leash and a long white stick. He had thick gray hair, very rumpled and wavy, and a wide smile.

He looked at Aref as if he could see him.

"Hello?" he said. "Is it Hayan?"

"No, it's Aref!" said Aref. "Hi! Are you Hugh? Did you have a good trip?"

The man laughed. "Yes, I did," he said. "And you are, excuse me . . . "

"I am your new neighbor, Aref! I was waiting for you. To come home, I mean. The Finnegans told me about you."

"You were waiting for me?" asked Hugh. "That's awfully nice. I like your voice."

Hugh reached out his hand toward Aref, and Aref shook it.

"Good handshake!" said Hugh. "And how old are you?"

"Eight," said Aref.

"Eight! Eight is a good year," Hugh said. "I remember it well. I am just a little bit older than you. By fifty years."

Aref asked, "You're fifty-eight?"

Hugh said, "Yep! Hayan, the boy I thought you might be, is ten. Now tell me about your family."

"My mom and dad are forty-three. Both of

them. They're going to school. That sounds weird! But my Sidi is much older than you."

"Where is your Sidi?" asked Hugh.

"He is back home in Oman. He's my grandpa."

"Oman. That must be an interesting place," said Hugh. "I never went there. But I wanted to. I went to Saudi Arabia."

Aref felt surprised. "You did? Why?"

"It was for my work," Hugh said. "I traveled to many places in my long, long life. Do you like to climb trees?"

Right away Aref's mind started swirling. Hugh had traveled to many places? How hard was that? Did Honeybun travel, too?

A blue car rolled into the parking lot very slowly. "That's my friend Robin!" said Aref.

"He's spending the night. We are going to make popcorn."

"It was very nice to meet you, Aref!" said Hugh. "Have fun and see you again."

Robin jumped out of the backseat with his rolled-up sleeping bag. Aref's father stepped out of their apartment to say hello to Robin's dad and welcome him.

"Look, Dad!" said Aref. "Hugh is back!"

"Hello, neighbor!" said Aref's dad.

Hugh and Aref's father shook hands. Then Robin's father shook hands with Aref's father and Hugh. Robin said hi. Hugh put his hand out to Robin, too. Suddenly there was a crowd. Honeybun pressed against Hugh's leg like a bodyguard.

"See you all later!" Hugh and Honeybun took off walking down the street toward

downtown. Hugh held Honeybun's harness and also tapped his long white cane. They walked very calmly.

Aref and Robin stared after them.

"That dog seems amazing," said Robin.

Robin Spends the Night

Aref was excited to have a friend for a sleepover. Back in Muscat, he and his best friend Diram used to dream up a lot of good ideas when they had overnights. They played ball in front of the house. They stared out the windows into the dark. They imagined they saw rockets flying. They joked a lot, and acted silly. They went with Aref's dad to get ice cream at a café down by the beach, and the

ice cream melted into their bellies and brains and gave them more good ideas. They stayed awake past midnight.

Now, in another world, Robin had thrown his stuff down on Aref's bed and was staring at Aref's empty terrarium. "Is that where your turtle will live?" he asked.

"I hope so," said Aref. "Maybe someday. We went to the pet store a few weeks ago, and they didn't have any turtles. They said they might be getting some in the fall."

"We could find one!" Robin said. "I saw one crossing my street last week. It was pretty big, though. It wouldn't fit in that thing."

Aref's father stepped into the room just then. "Does anybody want to take a walk to get some ice cream? I heard there is a

special kind here in Ann Arbor called Moon something?"

"Blue Moon!" Robin said. "It tastes like Froot Loops! They have it at Kilwins and the Creamery. I love the Creamery!"

"Let's go to the Creamery," said Aref's father. "We like that place."

"Froot Loops?" Aref couldn't remember ever eating Froot Loops, but he knew it was a rainbow-colored cereal. His mom said it had too much sugar. But you could get away with ice cream, now and then.

They stepped into the parking lot. Because it was evening, most of the cars were home, neatly lined up. Aref liked to compare them, memorize their names—Prius, Honda, Ford. It felt fun to have a friend over. You saw your place differently.

“Do you live in an apartment, too?” asked Aref.

“No, I live in a house,” said Robin. “It needs a new roof. The snow was so heavy last winter it broke part of our roof off.”

“That sounds exciting,” said Aref.

“It’s not,” Robin said.

Aref’s father was walking a little bit ahead of them. The trees were stretching their arms in loop-de-loops of soft evening shade.

“You know that dad who dropped me off?” Robin asked.

Aref nodded and kicked a white stone. He was thinking about how much snow it would take to break down a roof.

“He’s my second dad. I have two dads. A real one and a second one who is my stepdad, but he doesn’t like that word. Do you have

only one dad?" Robin picked up a stick and swiped it along the bushes they were passing.

"For sure! That's him!" Aref pointed at his father. His dad sometimes walked with a crooked little step, as if his foot hurt. He wore his baseball cap almost all the time now.

"Umm, where does your first dad live?" Aref asked.

"In Detroit. I go see him every other weekend."

"Is that fun?"

"Yes. Sometimes. Other times he's very strict and makes me go to bed early. He says he's tired. I have some sisters over there. They are babies. Twins."

"Twins! Do they cry at the same time?" Aref couldn't imagine having a sister, not to mention two.

"No! One cries, then makes the other one cry, then the first one stops crying. They do it with laughing, too. They are kind of like an echo back and forth. They look alike, too. Sometimes I'm not sure which one is which!"

Aref thought that sounded interesting. He had never met any baby twins.

"Do they sleep in the same bed?"

"No. They have two cribs. They wake each other up if they sleep together. Their names are Molly and Holly. I sleep on the couch."

Aref felt a slight blurring swoosh of air in front of their faces and Robin jumped, pointing at the sky. "A bat!"

"A bat?"

"Didn't you see it? It came really low!"

"It was so fast!"

"I love bats!"

“Me, too,” said Aref. “I just finished a book about them; it’s from the library! You could check it out next. In Oman we have fourteen species; they live in caves and sometimes in old buildings.”

“And under bridges,” said Robin. “I don’t know how many species we have in Michigan.”

“Probably a lot, since there are thirteen hundred thirty species in the world,” said Aref. “Did you know they love mangoes?”

“What is a mango?”

“You don’t have them?”

“I never heard of them.”

“It’s a fruit, like a papaya.”

“What’s a papaya?”

“You are joking me!”

For some reason they both started laughing

very hard. Aref's father slowed down and said, "What's so funny?"

"Robin doesn't know what a mango or papaya is!" said Aref.

Dad looked at Aref sharply. "You never laugh at people for things they don't know."

Aref felt surprised. "But he's laughing, too!"

"No," said Aref's father.

But Robin really *was* laughing.

"Tell Aref a food of Ann Arbor that *he* might not know," Aref's father said to Robin.

Robin looked a little confused.

"Think about it a minute."

Aref thought his dad was making this sleepover feel like school.

They waited at a corner. Aref pushed the walk button with his elbow.

"Do you know . . . paczki?" Robin said hesitantly.

"What?" asked Aref and his father at the same time.

"Paczki? It's a Polish doughnut! It has some jam inside it. They're the best! You have to get some!"

"I want one right now," Aref said.

"My grandparents were born in Poland so that means I'm part Polish. But you don't have to be Polish to eat them."

"Lucky for us!" said Aref's father.

For some reason that made Aref laugh. And then Robin laughed, too, and they were both sending laughter up into the evening air.

Stories in the Dark

Aref didn't like being high up on his bed while Robin slept on the floor, so he pulled his blankets and bedspread off his bed and curled up on the floor, too. This way they filled up almost the whole room.

"I like your rocks," Robin had said, pointing to Aref's rocks on the windowsill. "You really need to get a turtle because that thing"—Robin pointed at the terrarium—

"is weird just sitting there empty."

"I know. But there aren't any turtles in the pet store."

"You could put a gerbil in there," suggested Robin.

"A gerbil? I don't want a gerbil. Wait. Is that like a hamster?"

"Yup," Robin said. "It's also like a smaller guinea pig."

"But I don't want a pig," said Aref.

Robin started laughing really hard. "Can you imagine a pig in that glass tank? Or what about . . . a chicken?"

Aref laughed, too, then he was quiet. He said soberly, "It would be very bad to live in a glass tank."

Once, at the gold mall in Dubai, on a trip with his parents, he'd seen hundreds of fish

swimming around in a giant glass aquarium. The tank was bigger than Aref's whole house. Maybe it was bigger than this whole apartment building.

The shimmering fish, flashes of brown and green and blue, some with snouts, circled around trying not to look at all the people standing outside staring at them. Avoiding eye contact. What Aref remembered most was all the fish in the giant aquarium looked sad.

A riff of music came through the wall. A few notes, low then rising, then an up-and-down scale. "What's that?" Robin asked.

"It's Hugh playing his saxophone," said Aref.

Robin said, "I wish I could play an instrument."

"Me, too. Maybe we can learn!"

"I guess."

Robin sighed, and Aref changed the subject. “Do you have a grandfather?”

“Yes. A lot of them. One died.”

“One of mine died, too,” Aref said. “But I have another one and he is really great. I call him Sidi. That’s how we say ‘grandpa’ in Arabic. He is kind of like my best friend. Wait, how many grandfathers?”

Robin said, “Well, four total. But one is in a nursing home and one disappeared.”

“What?”

“Nobody knows where he went. He just disappeared from a gas station. They found his car. But we never saw him again. And he never came back to get his car.”

Aref was quiet for a moment, trying to imagine that happening to Sidi. “That’s horrible,” he finally said.

“It’s a mystery,” said Robin. “One of my dads still worries about it every day. No one knows. And my grandfather in the nursing home won’t talk. We think he can, but he doesn’t want to. My mom said he’s mad.”

“Who is he mad at?” asked Aref.

“Everybody,” Robin said. “I also have a few great grandfathers. They are really old. They can’t drive or anything.”

Suddenly it seemed to Aref he didn’t have many people in his own family at all. “My Sidi drives a jeep and took me to the desert,” he said. “We slept in a tent. He also let me sleep on his roof. We had a campout up there. The roof is flat.”

“You are lucky. Why didn’t he come with you here?” Robin asked.

“This is what I keep wondering.” Aref

sat up and punched his pillow into a better shape. “He says he can’t fly. Once we got to meet a falcon close up, in the desert. I even got to hold him.”

“But he doesn’t have to fly with wings; he could just get on an airplane, right?” Robin’s voice sounded sleepy.

“Right! But he won’t.”

“Tell him he will like Michigan,” Robin said.

Aref thought his friend had fallen asleep, but then he heard, “When we have Grandparents Day, he could come to our school.”

Sorry, Notebook, I Forgot About You for a Few Days

1. Paczki are delicious puffy little pillow doughnuts. Mine had blueberry jelly inside. But there are peach and cherry and other kinds, too.

2. Hayan and Layla can stand on their heads. The day after Robin slept over, I saw them outside on two yoga mats, and they were upside down. I can't do that.

3. Mom is doing exercises to make her fingers stronger. She has a squishy ball that she squeezes while she studies.

4. Hugh keeps two chairs outside in front of his door. His favorite sandwich is cheese and tomato, too. We sit by the big bush between our front doors and talk about things. He showed me how Honeybun obeys some commands. You can hardly hear the noise Hugh makes, but Honeybun hears. I asked him if everything is dark, and he said no. He said he sees inside his head. He sees in a different way. When he was a boy, he could still see with his eyes. He climbed a tree and looked down on everything. That's why he asked me, when we first met, if I liked climbing trees. But I never have! He also has echolocation, like a bat, which means he can feel sound bouncing off things and know how far away the things are.

5. Today when the mail truck pulled in, he heard it before I did.

First Day of School

By the time school started in September, they were not driving the red car anymore. Now they owned their own blue car. Pulling up in front of Martin Luther King Jr. Elementary School on Waldenwood Drive, Aref's dad said, "We're here!" Aref said bravely, "I'm not scared of anything at all." His mom said, "We're proud of you!" Actually he had a little floaty feeling in his tummy, like

a moth battering around a light bulb, but it was just an excited nervousness, not fear.

He'd been to arts camp, so he knew what the inside of the school looked like. He already had friends. He would get to see Ms. Liddy again, who would be his real art teacher during the school year. He would meet his new classroom teacher and everyone in his class. Hayan and Layla said the first day would be fun and everyone got a blue King T-shirt. They said, "People are so nice there. You'll see."

Aref was carrying a new plaid lunch box with a peanut butter and jelly sandwich, chips, carrots, celery, and an apple inside. Sidi, on the telephone yesterday, had wished Aref good luck with his new school year and said he was piling up presents for Aref that

would be waiting when he returned home. He'd found a stone on the beach that had a blue gem in the middle of it.

But Aref had a better idea. "Why don't you bring those presents to me?" he said.

Sidi laughed. "You know I can't! I am stuck here like my jeep in quicksand. I have to guard the fortress."

They had no fortress. The sultan had a fortress, but Aref and Sidi had never entered it. Aref knew Sidi was just kidding. The sultan also had a big white ship like a cruise ship.

Aref walked into King on the first day feeling brisk, tall, and energetic, as if he were a new sultan himself on the edge of a great adventure. In his classroom he found his own desk with his name written neatly

on a name card and—Robin was right—a blue T-shirt! There were eighteen students in the class. Aref was happy to see Jameela, who whispered, “Frankee’s in another class.” He wasn’t sure where Robin was. Everyone pulled their new school T-shirts on over their own clothes, so they already felt like a team!

I Always Wanted to Go There

Aref's teacher's name was Ms. Sullivan. She had a short red ponytail, a huge smile, and brown glasses. She asked her students to sit on the floor rug in a circle. She sat on a low stool with them.

She said, "Let's go around the circle and everyone say their name and then we all repeat it so we can start remembering, and then you say something you are *not*, then tell

us your family's country of origin—even if it is right down the street—because this year, in the magnificent third grade, we study the world!"

Aref was sitting between two girls with brown hair and deep brown eyes. They did not seem to be related, but they looked alike. He whispered to the one on his right, "Not? Something we are not?" She shrugged. Everyone around the circle was whispering. What did it mean exactly, something you were not?

"For example," Ms. Sullivan said. "I am *not* a hippopotamus. Right? I am not a seagull. I am not an ant living under a stone. But you don't have to use animals. You could say, 'I am not a broken chair.' Or 'I am not a potato chip.'"

Everyone laughed.

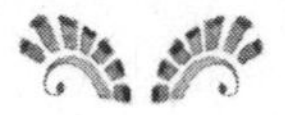

A boy across the circle said, "I want a potato chip. I am hungry!"

Ms. Sullivan smiled, then said, "I'll start, so you see how easy it is. I am Ms. Sullivan. I am proud to have an Irish background; my long-ago ancestors came to the United States from Ireland during the potato famine." *Just like the Finnegans next door!* Aref thought. Then Ms. Sullivan added, "And I am *not* the principal. And I am very excited to be your teacher this year."

Everyone laughed again.

"I am Petra," ("Petra!" they all repeated) said the girl to Aref's right. "And I am not a snowflake!"

Everyone laughed again. Petra said her country of origin was Turkey.

Ms. Sullivan stood up to poke a pin with a colorful head into each new mentioned spot on the big world map. Jameela said softly, "I came from Afghanistan and I am . . . not a shoe."

A boy named Ray said, "I came from the U.P., and I am not a bear. But we have a lot of them up there!"

Aref blurted out before he could stop himself, "The Upper Peninsula?"

Ray looked surprised that Aref knew about it. It was the secret part of Michigan way up high on the other side of the lake. "Yes!"

"Do you really have bears?"

"Yes, we do!"

Now Aref really wanted to go to the U.P.

A girl said, "I am Marielena, I came from Mexico, and I am not a doctor. But my father is."

Then it was Aref's turn and he hadn't even decided what to say yet, so he said, "I am Aref. ("Aref!" They all said it right, too. Because he had.) Then he paused a minute and said, "I am not a sea turtle, but I love them. And I come from Oman, a country where they live."

Ms. Sullivan smiled widely after Aref spoke and said, "Aref, welcome to King. I am glad you are in my class. I have always wanted to go to Oman—ever since I was a little girl. And someday I will." She poked a blue pin into Oman on the map.

"Why?" Aref asked, feeling flushed with pride.

"I read about Oman when I was little," Ms. Sullivan said. "Somewhere I found a long, fascinating story with lots of wonderful

pictures. I read about the mountains and the camels and the desert and the seashore and I just thought, that sounds like a place for me! We all have our dreams. So, you will have to tell me a lot about Oman this year. I have never before had a student from Oman."

Aref smiled as widely as he could. "I will tell you everything!" he said.

The girl on Aref's left, Dahlia, was from Greece, and she was not an eel. Lucy from Sri Lanka was not a cat. Kojo, a boy from Liberia, stayed quiet for a long minute, then said, "Not a lion!" and everyone jumped.

Ramin from Iran was not a jet plane. Joaquin from Mexico was not a train. Mahmoud from Morocco was not an olive. Regina from Argentina was not a dress.

King reminded Aref so much of his old

school back in Muscat. So many kids, born in so many places! Including Michigan. There were six students born in Michigan. They were not snowshoes, beavers, ping-pong balls, peanuts, elephants, or sailing ships.

Sidi, Where Are You?

1. I have so much to tell you! So today I am writing you a letter like the lists in my notebook.

My teacher is really good. Her name is Ms. Sullivan. She wants to come to Oman. Maybe you can be her guide, too. That is the second person I met who wants to go there. I already have friends.

2. We are doing poetry. First our teacher reads poems to us, then we write some. She said I am a good poet. She told us to keep our poems in a special notebook she gave us and all year we would be writing more. I might send you a few.

3. Poems are easy and fun and do not even feel like work. Lunch is fun every day, too. We sit at long tables just like back home. Ms. Sullivan plays Irish music on a CD for us at the very end of the day. She showed us how to dance a jig.

4. What are you doing? Mom's wrist is better, and Dad is good. We have a blue car. It is our own car now, not rented. I like Hugh next door. We made a game called 4 questions. He asks me four, then I ask him four. Maybe it should be called eight questions. They can be about anything. He asked me about you. He wants you to come visit us, too.

5. I asked if he can cook, since he is blind. He said of course he can, he is a chef, and he is going to invite us all to dinner soon.

Piles of Homework

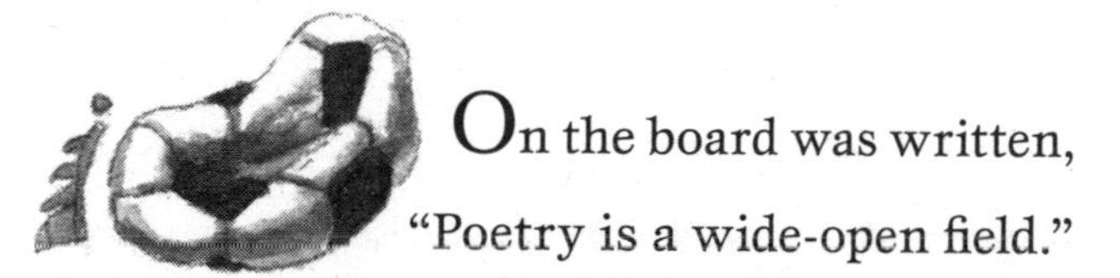

On the board was written, "Poetry is a wide-open field."

Ms. Sullivan started by asking them if they knew a word or two in a language besides English. Many of the students in the class knew more than one language already. Aref and Mahmoud spoke Arabic; Petra spoke Turkish; Ramin spoke Farsi; Dahlia spoke Greek; Marielena, Joaquin, and Regina spoke Spanish; Jameela spoke Dari; and the ones

who spoke only English knew a few words from other languages here and there, the same way Aref knew merci in French and guten tag in German.

Ms. Sullivan said, "We start with words. Then lines. Phrases. Sentences. Rhythms, like conversations." She read them several poems that mixed languages together. She said, "Poetry is like language soup, the taste of different flavors. Sometimes you just like the way a word sounds, pressed up against another word."

She said poetry was contagious. In a good way.

She read one poem that was half in English and half in Spanish.

It was by a poet named Lorca, and the poem had a lot of questions in it. You could

use questions in poems, and that would make writing even easier, since everyone knew how to ask questions. You could even ask questions of a desk, or a clock.

How much time is inside you?

Can you be late?

Dear desk, who else ever sat in you?

The whole board filled up with words and lists and questions. They were mixing it up, making lists for poems together. They were getting their brains rolling. And Ms. Sullivan also said they could write some things that were true and other things that were not true to make the poem funnier. She said, "Stretch!" There was nothing simpler than a list to get you started.

Class list of five words fun to say:

macaroni

hullabaloo

Humpty Dumpty

pooch

pinkie

Words from other languages we like:

Hasta la vista

Hasta luego

Ciao

Salaam

Tiempo

You could use any of these words in your poem, but you didn't have to. Ms. Sullivan put on some very nice music with no words while they wrote. She said it was from a YouTube

channel called Sad Cello, but Aref thought it was more peaceful than sad.

Aref wrote:

Waiting

Yallah means fast, quick.
It means get going, move!
Imshe also means go.
Imshe yallah is what my dad said
when a cat we didn't know
ran into our living room from the parking lot.
Yellow bird flies in circles
inside my head. I wanted to keep the cat.
Where are you today, cat?
It was spotted like an Arabian leopard.
I am waiting for something
to live in the tank in my room.

He wrote another poem, called "Brain."

Once there was a golden beach
everybody walked on.
It stretched from the sun to the moon.
It stretched from Muscat to Dubai,
from the soft sands to the purple mountains.
You could walk there by yourself
or with your favorite person
or with your whole family.
Kids made a hullabaloo.
The beach never said a word.
It was friendly to the waters, which
came and went
and never said anything either.
But you felt like the beach
and water talked to you.
You could carry them inside your brain.

They each picked one poem to share with the rest of the class. Carrie from Michigan wanted to read her list. She whispered it. Aref had no fear about sharing. He liked reading stories or poems out loud. They sounded better. The words felt close, and you went slower than you spoke when you just talked. Everyone listened carefully. Afterward they felt as if they knew one another better.

At the end of the week, Ms. Sullivan said, "I always like to start with poetry because we break the ice."

That was a phrase Aref did not know in English. What did it mean? He raised his hand to ask.

"It means we warm up and get to know one another. We get cooking," Ms. Sullivan said.

She also told the class that they had "piles of

homework for the weekend," and everybody looked worried. Then she laughed. She said, "Here it is: go home and make two lists. Write this down now, so you won't forget. One, what you hope for from your school year. Two, what you see outside your window." Then she clapped her hands together, smiled widely, called them "terrific poets!" and said, "Enjoy!"

Aref thought he was going to like school in the United States.

What I Hope for from My School Year

Friends

Soccer

Turtles

More turtles

Being neat

New Learning

Exciting Fun

What I See from My Window

Our blue car with a Michigan license plate
NCP 326
Parking places with no cars
Trees making things shady
A flattened soccer ball stuck behind a bush
Our neighbor Mrs. Finnegan staring at a squirrel
A blowing paper bag
and I will now go pick it
up to recycle

Listening In

Hayan said if you put your ear against a tree trunk, it would talk to you. He and Aref were standing outside Hugh's apartment where a big maple tree grew. Hugh was sitting in his chair with Honeybun curled up beside.

Hugh said he believed that. He said Honeybun probably did, too. "Maybe they hold their stories in their bark and their leaves," Hugh said.

So Aref snuggled up to the tree trunk and

wrapped his arms around it. “Hello?” he said.

“No, don’t talk,” Hayan said. “Just listen. You have to be very quiet to hear it.”

A postal truck paused and rumbled. Some jays flew over, making a loud squawking sound. Hugh laughed. Aref thought he heard the word *yes*. He said so.

“I agree. I think that’s what a tree says most often,” said Hugh.

“But why would it say yes?” asked Aref.

“It’s happy to be here,” said Hugh.

Hayan said he usually heard longer sentences, and sometimes they were in Arabic, like a prayer.

Aref stared at Hayan. “Did you know some bats are no bigger than a human thumb?” he asked. “Also, have you ever seen a tahr? It’s a

wild goat. We have a sanctuary for them back home."

He knew he was changing the subject, but he didn't know much about talking trees.

"Would you boys mind speaking a little Arabic for me?" asked Hugh. "I love hearing it. It carries me back to the days when I was young and traveling, walking the streets of great cities like Jeddah and Beirut and Damascus."

"My grandma lives in Damascus!" said Hayan.

"My dad went to Damascus!" said Aref.

"Walla!" said Hayan, and then they started talking in Arabic for Hugh and he rocked back in his metal chair smiling. Even Honeybun lifted her head and seemed to like it.

At first they said simple things to each other like, "What is your favorite food?" and "Do

you like school?" Hayan counted to twenty, and Aref said a poem about wild goats, since he had mentioned them. Hayan said he would sing a short song in Arabic if Aref would, too. Aref sang a song about the sun coming back every day, and Hayan sang a song about a tired donkey. Hugh started clapping.

Aref's father stepped out the front door. "Is this a concert?" he asked.

"Hugh likes to hear Arabic," Aref explained.

"It is a most melodious language, and it puts me in a good mood," Hugh said. "Also I like to hear Italian and French."

"Are these boys bothering you?" Aref's father asked.

"Never!" said Hugh. "And I would like to issue an invitation to dinner at my home next

Sunday night, to everybody. I will make a special meal for you."

Dad paused for a minute, thinking. Then he said, "We accept!"

Hayan said, "I will ask my parents!"

Dear Sidi,

Did you know trees can talk? I only heard one word. But Hayan heard a lot.

It seems like something you would know.

I was thinking about the wild goat sanctuary. We never went there, but we talked about it, remember?

Do you still think we could still go someday?

I found out there are bears in Michigan!

How are your computer classes? I love school here. I really do. My teacher is great.

Did you see Mish-Mish yet? Hope she is okay!

Love, Aref

HI AREF,

I AM TYPING IN BIG LETTERS. MY EYES LIKE THEM BETTER.

MISH-MISH IS FINE. SHE ASKED ABOUT YOU.

YOUR COUSINS WERE IN THE BACKYARD LOOKING FOR A LIZARD. THEY CAME INSIDE AND WE HAD LEMONADE. THEY SAID HI AND THEY SAID MISH-MISH SLEEPS WITH THEM.

I TOLD THEM ABOUT YOUR MESSAGES AND THEY WISH THEY COULD COME SEE YOU.

WE HAD A BIG SURPRISING RAINSTORM AND THE PARKING LOT AT LULU FLOODED.

THIS WAS THE SECOND STORM. THE LAST ONE MADE THOSE LOUD WATERFALLS.

I MISS YOU!

LOVE,

SIDI

Hugh's Gourmet Dinner

The fragrances of a delicious dinner floated out to the sidewalk and into the parking lot. Cinnamon, cumin, grilled tomatoes, jasmine rice . . . Hugh had left his front door open so they could all enter easily and the smells could emerge.

Hayan appeared in a white shirt, Layla in a frilly red dress. She set her mouse down on the arm of the couch. Aref was wearing his

blue tassel. All of the parents were dressed up. Aref's mother was carrying a plate of baklava she had made at home, now that her fingers could layer dough and bake again, and Mrs. Haddad carried a bottle of strawberry lemonade. It looked and felt like a real party.

Honeybun was sitting in a regal position beside a wooden rocking chair in the living room, staring at everyone calmly. The saxophone was standing up against the wall. Hugh, wearing a white apron, was at the stove stirring pine nuts in olive oil and garlic. The whole room smelled like back home.

"Hello, everyone, welcome! Ahlan wa sahlan!" Hugh smiled and waved toward his couch and chairs. Hugh liked saying a few words in Arabic, too. It made the adults smile.

The table was set with eight place mats,

four blue and four yellow. Checkered yellow-and-white cloth napkins were folded at each place, and large white plates were stacked in the kitchen. Mrs. Haddad asked if she could pour the lemonade, and Hugh waved her toward the ice maker on the outside of his refrigerator. Hugh's apartment was the same as Aref's apartment, but inside out and turned around.

Hugh had made a Moroccan stew with many vegetables, like green beans and yellow butternut squash, and spices, including saffron. He had lit a stick of sandalwood incense on the coffee table, another familiar smell—sandalwood trees grew in Oman. There were small glass plates of black Kalamata olives and sliced cucumbers and tomato salad on the table. There was a bowl

of crumbled white feta cheese. "It is a great pleasure to have my kind neighbors to dine at my table," Hugh said.

Then he asked everyone to fill their own bowls with jasmine rice, stew on top, and pine nuts on top of that. He passed a basket of flat, hot pita bread wrapped in a soft towel from one of the local Middle Eastern bakeries, which he had walked to pick up that very morning, with Honeybun at his side. He said, "Honeybun knows all the bakeries. In fact, that's how she got her name. One day, when she was beginning her guide dog training, learning how to follow instructions, she pulled a whole paper plate of honeybuns off a table and ate them before her trainer came back into the room. She got in a lot of trouble, and she also got her name. Luckily,

she's smarter than most dogs and she didn't get in trouble again, so she graduated."

Aref wanted to know how Honeybun acted on airplanes. "Happy," said Hugh. "Peaceful. As if she knows we're going somewhere else. Everything interests her. People's shoes. The different sounds. When she travels, her nose and ears are on high alert. And she is very protective of me."

Hugh asked the parents a lot of questions, like when he and Aref played the questions game. He asked exactly where they were born, if they had brothers and sisters. Hayan and Layla's parents were also students in the graduate program at the university, but they weren't sure they would return to Syria or Lebanon either, because of all the sad conflicts and problems always happening there. They

were thinking of staying in the United States or Canada, if they could get teaching jobs and proper visas.

Aref felt a swoop of panic. What if his parents decided not to go home either? He cast a worried look at his dad, who was listening carefully to Mr. Haddad.

Then Aref's mother asked Hugh about his family and he told about his sister Nancy who lived in Arizona and ran the lumberyard. She was blind, too, and everyone seemed amazed that she could do such a big job with so many employees, and loads of lumber and trucks arriving to pick it up all the time. "We have been best friends since we were very small," Hugh said. "We both had our sight then, but lost it gradually to a disease inherited from our grandmother, whom we loved so much.

My sister lost her sight first, in her late teens, me in my early thirties. We had to get used to our new worlds. But I kept traveling. I guess I could move to Arizona and live right next door to her, but I like the chilly winters of Michigan, too, and my last job was here, so I stayed. At least I see her for three months every year. And we talk on the phone almost every day."

Aref noticed that he said "see her," which seemed odd and also not. Hugh used that word often.

Then they all talked about "home" and what made "home," and did we need our closest friends and relatives near us to feel at home? Aref's mom and dad said home could be everywhere; at least they were trying to believe this. Hugh said he had always believed

this, too, since his early life of traveling. As long as we were comfortable with ourselves, and a little flexible, we could find new homes easily. Hayan and Layla's parents said they did not think they could ever feel truly at home in America, but they were really trying. They said, "It helps us to have you all here," and they gestured to Aref's parents, which surprised him. He was interested in this discussion, but Hayan and Layla were whispering about Honeybun and moving the salt and pepper shakers around.

Everyone loved the dinner and served themselves to second helpings from the big stew pot.

Hugh was happy. He said, "That is the mark of a good dinner, when I can hear the spoon hitting the empty pot."

"How did you learn to be such a great cook?" Aref's mother asked.

"I live by myself! Who else would cook for me? Not Honeybun!" answered Hugh.

Everyone laughed.

"And I was a professional chef back in my twenties, too, between traveling jobs," Hugh added.

No one mentioned that Hugh made such beautiful food despite being blind. Sometimes Hugh could see better than anyone.

One Thing

Aref's father had a new theory. "Every day, focus on one thing. Think about it, examine it, look at it from different directions, change your mind. Make notes, ask questions, connect it to other things if you want but still . . . mostly one thing."

Really? How could anyone possibly do that? Today Aref's father was thinking about new studies regarding palm trees. He was taking a lot of notes.

What should his one thing be, Aref wondered.

He was no longer afraid of not making friends. He was no longer scared of feeling strange. Nothing was strange. One day at school, Regina had started crying, embarrassed by something she thought she had done wrong, but Ms. Sullivan said, “It’s okay! It’s okay to do something different. Don’t worry if you feel strange. Everybody might feel a little strange every day, for a whole day or maybe just for a minute. Because life is full of mysteries and we keep trying to figure them out. Feeling strange can make us more creative. Who else feels strange?”

Many people raised their hands. Aref didn’t.

Maybe Aref’s one thing was, remembering?

He felt it was his job not to forget where he came from. No one else in his class had ever seen Oman. No one else had held a falcon. Sometimes he felt as if Oman were living inside his own body, like blood, like bones, it seemed so close. Sometimes when he awakened, he forgot entirely he was in Michigan and looked out the window expecting to see the Arabian Sea in the distance.

Hiking for Turtles

On a Saturday in golden late October, after their regular school-year classes were ticking along and life seemed somewhat settled again, Aref's father surprised him by saying, "Today we are going to the Nichols Arboretum trails to take a hike. Sound good?"

"Very good!" said Aref. "Maybe I will climb a tree!"

His mother was in the kitchen packing

sandwiches, constructing a picnic. She was wearing blue jeans and a University of Michigan T-shirt, a new outfit for her. Dad was wearing his Michigan hat, so Aref ran to get his, too.

Aref's mother put a big sack of lentil chips in the picnic bag. "We bought some chocolate for the journey!" she said. "Come help me, habibi; you can wash the apples."

Aref was good at washing things. He stood on the short stool in front of the sink and used a colander. He could see Mrs. Finnegan outside on her patio watering her plants. He waved at her. He held up an apple.

On the floor of the backseat of the car, Aref spotted an apple core he had dropped about a week before. It had rolled under the seat

forgotten. Now it was a shriveled apple mummy. He picked it up, stared at its shrunken shape, then tossed it outside under the bush beside their apartment to a waiting squirrel who was happy to get his breakfast delivered. Aref was starting to think the squirrel knew him. The squirrel had stared through his bedroom window one day, his furry face pressed against the glass. Aref wished he could invite him in to poke around. He called the squirrel "Buster."

The arboretum trail was located by the Huron River. Aref had heard about it, but they hadn't been there yet. He was excited to hike beside the river.

They parked in the shade, leaving their picnic in a cooler with ice in the car.

To depart the world of people and enter the

world of chirps, rustles, shadowy signals . . . pockets of mud from the last rain . . . stones in a heap . . . mushrooms . . . twigs shaped like alphabet letters . . . sweeter world of birds and dirt and secret nests and rough bark toughened by years . . . was really something. There was no chatter but forest chatter. It was a better world, to be so quiet you could hear it all. No one else was there.

"There's a big football game today, lucky for us," Aref's dad whispered. That meant everybody was at home watching television or at the stadium watching the game.

Aref ran ahead of his parents. His personal trail curved right to left, side to side, in a figure eight pattern. Then he tiptoed slowly to listen to the chirping and crackling. He circled back to his parents. "I see a tree to climb!" He

stepped into the low crook of a welcoming tree. He hugged it around its trunk, like hugging a person around the waist. Two brown caterpillars were crawling up its bark. They blended in. Aref stepped carefully two branches higher. He felt peaceful and happy. "Sidi would love it here!" Aref called down to his parents.

Back in Oman, when he and Sidi walked alongside the Arabian Sea, they felt calm. It was their tradition. Some days they walked a long time without speaking. Other days they jabbered nonstop. When you walked by water, you felt connected to other places that the same water touched, other realms where water was flowing. The water was bigger than you were. It was a system, whole worlds of fish and creatures, water plants and microbes swirling

and interacting. You were just looking at the top of it. Maybe water owned the earth.

"He really would," said Aref's father. Aref had jumped down from the tree and was brushing off his hands.

"I think we should try again," said Aref's mother. "To get him to come here. He could buy a plane ticket, lock his house, take a taxi to the airport, and stay with us for three months. Easy! Can you imagine him tromping along here with us on a Saturday morning? I can."

"Like Hugh going to Arizona," said Aref.

"Exactly. Why is he so stubborn?" said Aref's mother.

"Because he's scared," said Aref's father.

"Sidi is never scared of anything!" protested Aref.

"That's what you think," Aref's father said.

“What’s he scared of?” Aref didn’t believe it.

“Microwave ovens, for one thing.”

“Really? He just says they’re not necessary.”

“No,” said Aref’s father. “He’s *scared* of them. He says they’re from outer space and no food should get hot that fast. He also seems to be scared of getting the messages out of his telephone—like maybe the telephone will bite him.”

A very large white bird like an egret or a crane flew right in front of them then, landed gently in the reeds, and turned its long beak in their direction.

“Look at that!” said Aref’s mother. She loved birds. She loved stories about birds, poems about birds, paintings of birds. Birds had wide lives. They were not tied to clocks or calendars. They had schedules imprinted

in their brains, though—when to migrate, when to gather twigs to build a nest.

"Yes! Talk him into it!" Aref could not imagine anything better than sharing Ann Arbor with his favorite person, Sidi, who had only been out of Oman one other time in his whole life, to go to Dubai.

"That bird has a nest, look! Right on the edge of the water, all those woven twigs and grasses, look!" Mom was still occasionally holding her hand gently, as if it were a delicate moth wing, but her fingers could point.

As they stepped closer to look at the nest, Aref noticed the familiar bulky shapes of turtles drifting and dipping under the water, near the bank. He trembled with excitement, pointing, "Look! Turtles! Here's where they are! We found them!"

Dozens of turtles, mixing and mingling and gliding!

“That’s what I heard! This place has turtles!” said Aref’s father happily. “I didn’t want to mention it in case we didn’t see any!”

Eastern box turtles with orange maps on their backs, red sliders bearing fancy ear markings, painted turtles circling and diving. The happy turtles seemed to be gathered around a fallen half-submerged trunk of a massive tree, weaving in and out of the soggy bark. This was turtle paradise! One small red-eared slider was sitting on a half-sunken branch, sunbathing.

Aref knew, from his “Know Your Michigan Turtles” brochure, that Michigan’s state reptile was the painted turtle. Its back shell, imprinted with orange and yellow markings,

looked like it had gone to arts camp. He knew that Michigan was home to ten native turtle species, and he also knew that World Turtle Day was May 23. He was already looking forward to it, though it was a long time away.

Jameela had told him that Ann Arbor had a parade for World Turtle Day. "You can walk down the street with a green turtle puppet tied to your head. Some people, even grown-ups, make different kinds of turtle costumes. This year my brother and I want to make big cardboard signs about being kind to turtles. Can you help us? Because you said you have met the really big turtles!"

Aref had agreed to help. It was nice to live in another place on Earth that knew turtles were important.

You Could Take a Little One

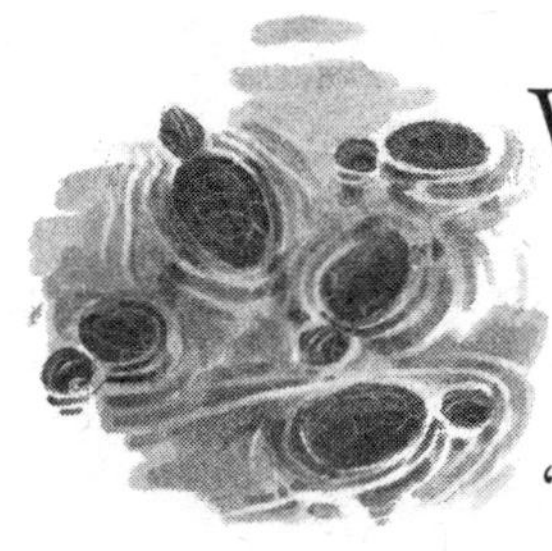

When it was time to leave the river and eat their picnic, Aref's mother said, "We could come back here with a net or a jar. Dad could lean in and snatch a little turtle. Then we wouldn't need a pet store!"

Aref looked at his mother in horror. He had just been staring with great affection at the happy little turtles swimming circles around their parents. One of the parents had lifted its head and looked him straight in the eyes.

How could his mom say that?

The little turtles and bigger turtles seemed so content together paddling among the muddy reeds and sticks by the side of the bank, swimming up and out and back in, dipping into the river reeds and grasses, in a graceful routine.

"What? Take them from here and put them into that little glass tank in my room? Take them from their mothers and fathers?"

How could she say this?

Take them from the water when they obviously loved water?

"Mom, *look* at them!" Aref said.

It seemed shocking that a *mother* could suggest this.

What would a turtle feel like, to be suddenly transplanted into a tight glass rectangle with a few plastic toys in it? What a horrible idea!

Then she said something even worse: “But it would be free!”

That was the exact opposite! Then it *wouldn’t* be free!

Aref knelt down. The turtles skedaddled farther off into the water. Aref made a looming shadow over their light.

“Don’t get too close,” his father said. “Don’t fall into the river! I need to research these turtles. Shouldn’t they be hibernating soon?” he added.

This was a good question. Some hibernated; some didn’t. They would both look it up and maybe they could visit the turtles again right when they woke up in the spring.

The river smelled of mud and sunlight, deep fishy places, stones and weeds. There was also a dank smell like rotten wood. A fisherman was floating in a boat out toward the other bank. He raised his hand to them. Just like in Muscat, fishermen were friendly. Aref waved back.

They hiked to the picnic tables near the start of the trail and unpacked their lunches. Aref's mother had bought a little checkered tablecloth like the one they used back home in Oman when they ate out in the yard. They were starving. They gobbled every bite of the chocolate.

DEAR AREF,

HOW IS MY BOY?

ARE YOU HAVING FUN?

DO YOU EVEN REMEMBER ME?

I SAW YOUR FRIEND DIRAM. HE WAS HAVING A RACE WITH HIS LITTLE GIRL COUSINS ON THE BEACH. DIRAM WAS WEARING HIS MONKEY FACE SHIRT, THAT'S HOW I KNEW HIM.

HE CAME AND TALKED TO ME AND SAID TO TELL YOU HI!

I LIKED YOUR REPORT ABOUT THE TURTLES.

SOME THINGS ARE BIGGER IN AMERICA

AND SOME THINGS ARE SMALLER. SO THE TURTLES ARE SMALLER.

DO THEY SPEAK ONLY ENGLISH?

I WOULD LIKE TO SEE THE TURTLE WITH A YELLOW MAP ON ITS BACK.

THE SUN IS SHINING. IT'S STILL VERY HOT. LIZARDS ARE SINGING SONGS IN MY GARDEN.

EVERYTHING IS THE WAY YOU REMEMBER IT AND EVERY DAY I MISS YOU A LOT.

LOVE,

SIDI

Empty

That night, before he took his bath, Aref realized his skin smelled green, like forests and rivers, and slightly yellow, too, like sunshine. He shook some smooth gray rocks out of his pocket and lined them on the windowsill between the two crystal rocks he'd brought from home.

What a great day, hiking with his parents. Except for the near-kidnapping-of-baby-turtle incident. Why didn't they do this more often?

Just go out and walk around? Because everyone was always working or studying!

His father had said they would go to Independence Lake Park soon, only twelve miles from Ann Arbor, where there was a real beach. A lake beach. And someday soon they would drive to Lake Michigan for a holiday. They would stay in a cabin.

Aref stretched out under his sheets, staring at the empty terrarium next to his bed. He smiled.

The plastic palm tree and yellow water bowl, waiting patiently, inside glass.

He had changed his mind. He no longer wanted a turtle in his room.

Finding a Quote You Like and Writing Something About it (Homework)

"Every elephant has to carry his own trunk."
—Proverb from Zimbabwe

I saw this quote on a bulletin board at the ice cream shop. While my dad was paying for chocolate almond ice cream cones for Hayan and me, I saw it and said, "Dad, take a picture of this!" Hayan asked why, and I told him about our homework. He

thought it sounded like easy homework. He said, “But what are you going to write?” and I said, “Maybe it’s like everybody has to carry something. And right now I am carrying ice cream! Also I like the word *Zimbabwe*.”

First Snow Came Secretly Whispering

You don't know when it's coming. It sneaks up on you like a dream. Sometimes it comes when you are sitting in the classroom writing numbers in a row. Everyone looks up, and the whole day has changed. We rise up and float to the windows. Sometimes it comes when you are snoozing, wrapped in your sheets and blankets. You awaken, surprise! What was brown is white. What was concrete

is soft. The parking lot is now a giant page. Little leaves coated with icing.

Aref shouted with joy when he saw it. "It's here!" He was the first person up that day. It was a Saturday, his mom and dad still sleeping. Hugh told him later that he heard him yelping through the wall and thought maybe Aref had fallen out of bed. His parents came hopping into the hallway. "What, habibi, what?"

The first snow came secretly whispering around the midnight hour, and the season shifted from fall to winter. All across Ann Arbor, the boots started humming in closets and the sleds started shivering and hoping for someone to remember they were waiting, waiting, to glide.

Aref was stuck to the front window,

pointing. "Look, look, it happened, it snowed!"

He opened the front door and ran out onto the white sidewalk in his socks. Of course his socks instantly got wet. Somehow he hadn't thought of snow as being *wet.*

He twirled in place. He was the first person to step in this patch. Every footprint was his. His page.

His mom stood in the doorway, shivering in her bathrobe, clutching it closed in front of her, and smiling. She had never seen snow either. Snow is one of the miracles of the world.

Dear Sidi,

It's white here now. The snow came down. It's magic. You wouldn't believe it.

The snow makes me think of the desert when we woke on our campout and the birds were singing and out in front of us everything was golden, so different from the dark night before. Remember? How everything changed?

I don't think you could wear your sandals here, though—you would have to get boots. I got blue ones.

At school some of my friends were riding two sleds down a hill and having a contest. I fell off. But it didn't hurt, because I fell into the snow and it's soft. Did Dad send you a picture?

What are you doing?

At the Oasis Grill they are making za'atar

bread more often to celebrate the snow. They serve Arabic coffee in the little cups that you like. I mean it, you would feel good here.

Love,

Aref

HI MY BOY!

BE CAREFUL ON THAT SLED! NO MORE BROKEN ARMS! MONSIEUR SAYS HE WANTS TO RIDE A SLED, TOO. CAN A JEEP RIDE A SLED?

NOTHING IS HAPPENING HERE. NO, THAT'S WRONG. EVERYTHING IS HAPPENING.

BUT I JUST DON'T CARE ABOUT IT AS MUCH. OH! THIS IS MY PROBLEM, NOT YOURS. SORRY. YOUR OLD SIDI LOSES HIS WAY SOMETIMES.

WHERE IS MY NAVIGATOR? THE FRONT SEAT OF MONSIEUR IS VERY EMPTY. THE OTHER DAY I BOUGHT A BIG BAG OF ORANGES AND PUT THEM IN THE FRONT SEAT LIKE MY PASSENGER, WHERE YOU USED TO SIT. THEN I PUT THE SEAT BELT ON THEM.

THERE WAS NO ONE BUT ME TO LAUGH.

LOVE,

SIDI

No Bullies

Aref had wondered why his school had an anti-bullying club, since he hadn't met a single bully in the school halls or cafeteria yet.

He asked Ms. Sullivan about it. "Excuse me, umm, where are the bullies?"

She laughed. "Maybe we don't have many because we're aware of them! We try to pay attention so it doesn't happen too much. We talk about it. Keep our eyes open. Maybe you

should join that club; it's a good club. You learn important skills for your life and your future. Grown-ups can be bullies, too, you know."

She looked sad when she said that.

"It's a skill for life, dealing with bullies," she said.

Aref felt lucky he had never met a grown-up bully personally. He had only seen them on TV.

Although one day he and his dad saw two men shouting at a bus stop by the pizza parlor. One was swinging his fist. Maybe he was a bully.

The club met on Tuesdays after school. Aref asked his parents if he could go.

His mom acted worried. "Why, my love? Is this something you think about? Is someone bullying you? Why would you want to go?"

"I want to be ready just in case," Aref replied.

"I want to know about it. I want to help."

Sometimes there were bullies in the animal kingdom. An otter could eat a heron. But that was called the natural order of things. People ate cows and chickens. Aref was thinking about being a vegetarian like Annie in his class because he really did not like eating a piece of chicken and thinking, *This was somebody's leg. This is a dead body*. The worst thing he had ever heard of was *turtle soup.*

The best thing about the anti-bullying club was that the first graders ran it. Their teachers trained them in the serious but simple principles of RECONCILIATION, like getting along, and RESTORATIVE JUSTICE, like making things a little more fair, and COMPROMISE, like sharing. Those were big words for first graders! Aref was impressed. He had to learn them too.

But with first graders in charge, everyone listened better. No one argued with them. If fifth graders had a fight or one told another their hair was ugly and made them cry, they were called into a session with the first-grade team who sat them down and asked a lot of questions and listened carefully, then asked what they might do to make things better. They were the MEDIATORS.

"Tell us what happened," they said seriously to the people who had been fighting. "One person talks, then the other person. No interrupting. Everyone has to listen," the mediators instructed.

They gave some ground rules. Aref liked that term. GROUND RULES, as if you were telling the ground what to do.

The third and fourth graders (who were

allowed to sit in and offer comments afterward) thought the first graders seemed really small, but smart. Lyda and Angus, the first graders in charge that day, weren't afraid to speak up. A teacher sat off to the side in case anybody needed help, but the first graders were very brave.

Lyda asked a fourth grader why he made fun of a girl's lunch and made her cry. The fourth grader named Tonio looked so sad. Then he whispered, "Because I wanted it. It looked better than mine."

Another day a fourth grader named Sharif apologized to a third-grade boy named Assef because he had made fun of him for being an Arab.

Aref didn't understand this problem. Wasn't the fourth grader an Arab, too?

He said he was an Egyptian. Aref thought Egyptians *were* Arabs. And also, *he* was an Arab. It was a great thing to be! This was confusing. Usually Aref never thought about such things much. You had to be *something.*

Later, when he got home, Aref told his mom, "It's nice because we get to have first-grader friends. You know, when you're older, you usually don't."

One day a boy named Lucas chased Aref after class and punched him in the arm, saying Aref had taken his pen.

"What?" asked Aref. He had not taken anyone's pen.

"I saw you writing with it!" Lucas yelled. "Give it back, it's mine!"

Aref pulled the blue University of Michigan

pen his dad had given him out of his backpack pocket. “This one?”

“Yes,” Lucas said, grabbing it. “That’s mine. You stole it.”

“I didn’t take it! My dad gave it to me. Yours is right there in the side of your backpack!” Aref could see Lucas’s pen stuffed in the water bottle pouch with some papers. He pulled it out himself.

Lucas was shocked. “Oh!”

He gave Aref his pen back, “Mine is just the same,” he said.

“You punched me!” said Aref.

“I’m sorry,” said Lucas.

Aref said, “Okay,” and never told anyone else what had happened.

If Lucas had not apologized, he might have gone to the anti-bullying club for help.

My Focus

1. I want to do a good job.

2. I want to be neat.

3. Sometimes if my brain feels messy, I try to make something else neat, like my desk.

4. Then my brain feels better, too.

I am really interested in the human skeleton. Dad took me into an anatomy lab at the university and it was full of bones and charts. It made me think about how everything inside my body is really neat. The way it all fits

together. It's so odd how we never see it.

But if a person is upset, they could think about that. How things are still attached. And the blood is still flowing.

Every Day Is a Holiday

"We wish you a Merry Christmas!" Suddenly bright music was playing in all the stores. "Joy to the world!" It even seemed like it was playing in the streets.

Aref learned that schools in the United States took the Christmas holiday very seriously. They closed for two or three weeks. And every day felt like a party, a festival, a celebration, for weeks before that.

The windows of the stores in Ann Arbor all changed. Lots of shining! Pine trees dazzled with red balls, strings of lights, tinsel.

The second graders were collecting cans of food for their project, to make gift bags for hungry people. The kindergarten students did a reindeer parade through the school halls, under dangling glittery silver stars.

Because Aref's school was such an international school, the teachers took time to talk about special holidays such as Kwanzaa, Ramadan, Eid al-Adha, Hanukkah, Passover, Diwali, Bodhi Day, and Vesak (the Buddha's Birthday), in different religions and cultures. Suddenly it seemed every day was a holiday, and you would have to work hard to find a regular day anywhere.

Aref didn't remember his old school liking

holidays quite this much, but it was fun to learn about them. Each day felt full of surprises. Candy canes, small packets of star stickers on every desk. Who was Santa, exactly? He lived up north, in the direction of the polar bears of Manitoba. He was a generous hero. He had different names all over the world, and anytime you gave something away, you were a little like Santa yourself. He reminded Aref of Sidi.

Lucy, from Sri Lanka, said her family was Buddhist, and most people in their class would probably not know about things like the Hungry Ghost Festival or the Festival of the Tooth. Tooth? A temple held a little piece of the Buddha's tooth. You could never see it, but people celebrated it. In that way, Aref thought, the tooth was a little like the sultan

back home. He had never seen him, but he heard of him all his life.

In his classroom they were doing "Secret Friend" presents, but the gift could not cost more than three dollars. Aref needed to buy a present for Ray from the Upper Peninsula. He had drawn Ray's name out of a hat. Ray had a ponytail. Aref glanced around the room slyly. He wondered who had drawn his name.

At home his mother bought a big rosemary plant in a pot, put it on the side table, and folded some paper cranes to hang from it, like in Japan. Christmas was not really their usual holiday, but why not celebrate everything?

She had the idea that they would give only one gift to each other on Christmas Day. This meant that Aref needed to find a gift for both his mother and his father. He counted his

money. He had seventeen dollars and forty-two cents. After buying his Secret Friend gift, he would have fourteen dollars and forty-two cents.

His father offered to walk with him to the dollar store and wait outside so Aref could shop in private.

For Secret Friend Ray, Aref bought a really nice set of colored pencils.

For his mom he bought a set of rainbow-colored dishcloths for the kitchen.

For his dad he bought a very large chocolate bar.

When Aref came back outside, a man wearing a puffy blue coat was holding a red bucket and ringing a bell, right next to his dad. His father motioned to him that he could drop some money into the bucket if he wanted to.

He was feeling a little attached to the small amount of money he had left, but he took a deep breath and dropped in a whole dollar.

Aref loved how the world seemed twice as lit up during December. Stringing colorful lights everywhere was such a fine idea. Why not leave them up all year? Too much electricity?

Aref's secret friend, Mahmoud, gave him a handmade wooden box that was so beautiful he could not believe it had only cost three dollars.

The Happiest Day, The Saddest Day

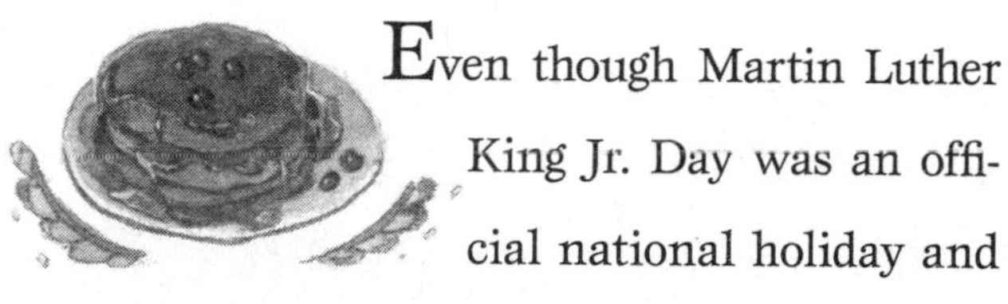

Even though Martin Luther King Jr. Day was an official national holiday and school was closed, King was hosting a special birthday party. They had to! He was the precious patron saint of the school.

For two hours in the middle of the day, the school would host an MLK peace and justice parade, and some presentations at the gym. Parents were invited.

Aref had chosen to read a poem about freedom and dreams by Langston Hughes. Ms. Sullivan invited him to read because his poem voice was so strong. When he practiced with the microphone, his voice rolled out in waves. This was thrilling!

Jameela, who was often shy, would be singing a peace song from South Africa. She would be singing a cappella, all by herself without instrument accompaniment, which everyone thought was very brave. Other students were doing a few different things—there would be a reading of the school's own peace and justice proclamation, a three-student presentation by fifth graders about the life and work of Dr. King, a song from India about the Great Horizon, and lots more.

Everyone dressed up. Aref was wearing his

Omani hat and his blue tassel, those precious last presents Sidi had given him before they left for the United States. He wore a white shirt, because the tassel looked best against it.

Dr. Martin Luther King, Jr., had been a true hero, for his time, for all time. He belonged to the people of the United States, but also he belonged to the whole world—to anyone who believed in the principles he stood for, peace and justice, freedom and respect. Aref's class had been talking about him for the whole week! The students were proud to go to a school named after Dr. Martin Luther King, Jr.

Aref had been the only one in the class who knew that Martin Luther King had jumped out a second-story window as a child, when he heard his grandmother died. Ms. Sullivan said, "You specialize in the unusual details,

my friend." He had written this fact on one of his discovery lists when he was still in Oman, after his class back home also did research on Dr. King.

And now, the big day!

Why was it, when the sun was shining, your mind felt shinier, too?

Aref's parents were cooking breakfast *together,* which was rare. Usually just one of them cooked it. Dad was chopping green onions into very tiny pieces to grill them in butter in a skillet before mixing in scrambled eggs and Mom was stirring whole-wheat pancake batter with blueberries in a yellow bowl.

They were laughing in the tiny kitchen, bumping into one another, mixing Arabic and English. They even had violin music playing on the radio. Earlier they had listened to Dr.

Martin Luther King, Jr.'s most famous speech.

"Why didn't you wake me up?" Aref asked. He had listened with his classmates to the speech at school already, on January 15, Martin Luther King's actual birthday, and they had talked about it. But he wanted to hear it again. "I have a dream. . . . "

"We need to think about our dreams every single day," Ms. Sullivan had said. "We need to work for our dreams. No matter what age we are. It's never-ending."

A dream didn't just come along and pick you up, like a taxi.

After breakfast Aref and his parents walked to school. The weather was bitingly cold, but brilliant. They wore their new thick American coats. Aref's was blue.

Aref's father said, "Aref, when I was in third grade, I never spoke to the whole school through a microphone, not once. I don't think we even had a microphone. It is a great honor to be selected. We are so proud of you." He put his arm around Aref's shoulder and hugged him to his side. Aref smiled.

"Are you scared?" his mother asked.

Aref felt a bubble of fizz in his tummy and throat, but he was not scared.

Kojo and his dad drove past them and Kojo's dad honked. He called through the window, "Want a ride?" and Aref's dad said, "Thanks so much, we prefer to walk today!"

Kojo waved and Aref waved back.

In the parade, the first graders carried balloons and banners. Second graders beat oatmeal-box drums they had made in art class.

The third graders sang, and the fourth and fifth graders did everything—sang, twirled, waved, and greeted people.

Robin rode a unicycle alongside the big plowed snowbank by the side of the road. He waved, too. Everyone was in a good mood.

Saying the poem from the stage, Aref felt bigger. His own voice was speaking, but also it was Langston's voice and Martin's voice and every person who had ever had a dream. Backstage, Ms. Sullivan hugged him tightly. "That was *perfect*!" she whispered.

Walking home, Aref felt proud of how he had read the poem. His hands didn't shake. He'd held the paper in both hands, waist-high, but he knew the poem by heart, so he'd kept his head up for eye contact with the audience.

People in the audience had smiled at him. The microphone didn't "pop." He didn't "swallow any words."

Now he watched himself go by in a shop window. His Omani hat perched proudly atop his head made him look taller. A lot of people had complimented his hat.

His parents, walking a few paces behind him, suddenly got the giggles. They started laughing so hard that Aref turned around and put his arms up in the air. "What?"

"Your father is a funny man," his mother said.

"Your mother is funnier," said his father.

"We are more proud of you than we could ever be of ourselves," said his mother.

"But why did you laugh?" asked Aref.

His mother said, "Because we are happy

and we love you. Because we can't believe you did that. You're so brave! Because we're full of relief that you're doing so well here."

Aref turned and stared at them, walking backward. "I'm doing well?"

"Better than we are! And we're happy for you! We love all your friends. Don't fall in that big heap of snow!"

He would always remember their laughter because of what happened next.

Back in the apartment, Aref's father opened his email and learned the terrible news.

Sultan Qaboos, the leader of their country of Oman for all their entire lives, was dead.

Peace Be Upon Him

Aref stood at his father's elbow, staring at the computer screen. What had happened? The sultan was only eighty. Sidi was one year older than that.

"Bless his heart, bless his soul, peace be upon him, how could this be?" Aref's father took his hands from the keyboard and put his elbows on the table and covered his eyes. "Oh," he said, softly. "Oh. I just hate being

away from home when this happens."

Since the sultan had no children, he had personally picked the next person to be in charge of Oman and placed that person's name into a long white envelope. Probably it would be one of his three cousins, Assad, Haitham, or Shihab.

"Rest his soul," Aref's mother said. "What a good, good man. He really loved us."

Everyone said Sultan Qaboos had "brought Oman into the twentieth century." Sidi had told Aref he actually saw, with his own eyes, all the roads of the country being paved! These were the same roads that he drove Monsieur on now. Sidi had seen all the wires on giant spools when electricity was installed, even in villages. It wasn't that long ago. The sultan wouldn't allow tall skyscrapers to be built, as in Dubai,

since he loved the view of his mountains too much, so people built short hotels.

He protected the turtles—Aref liked that especially about him. He welcomed visitors from other countries. Before Sultan Qaboos, Oman didn't have many visitors.

He tried to establish peace when there were international quarrels. He was known as a tolerant peacemaker. He had allowed temples and churches for other religions besides Islam to be built—Buddhist and Christian and Hindu, for example—to serve residents from other countries. And he never stood high on a podium and said, "Look at me." Even though his picture hung in many buildings, most people never saw him. He was humble. Maybe he was shy.

He loved art, classical music and culture in

general. The Muscat Cultural Festival lasted a whole month. Most of it happened outside, for free, so Aref had been going to it with his parents and Sidi for his whole life. Different events every night. Plays and movies. Basket weavers wove baskets and showed you how to do it. People danced in ancient, tribal circles, with scarves. Children played violins, cellos, and flutes from a stage. Sultan Qaboos supported good works and environmental preservation and science and exploration. And now he had died.

For the rest of the day, Aref's mother and father were glued to the computer, reading updates, sending messages to their colleagues at the university back home. Aref kept thinking about how the day had changed. The happiest day had become the saddest day.

That night, after eating a little cold supper of hard-boiled eggs, za'atar spice, cucumbers, and pita bread, Aref lay awake in bed tugging at his pajamas to straighten them, staring at the ceiling, and thinking about home. He could hear the low voice of a television through the wall, from Hugh's living room. He wondered what Hugh was watching. Somebody had left a glass jar of daisies at their front door. He wondered if it was Hugh.

Maybe Oman would never be the same.

The flag would be lowered for forty days. Thousands of people would stand in the streets praying as the processional carrying the sultan's casket rolled past. And Aref and his parents would not be there to pay their respects.

Aref's father was right. It *was* hard to be so far from home when big things happened.

Instead of One Thing, Do Another

To lift their spirits the following Saturday, Aref and his parents went to Nichols Arboretum, inviting Layla to come along with them. Hayan had gone skating, but Layla didn't like skating. She said, "I fell on my bottom once and it hurt for a week."

Layla wore her hair in two braids. She wore a pink coat and a purple hat and was carrying her mouse in an extra mitten to keep it

cozy. "Have you ever lost your mouse?" Aref asked her in the car. She said yes, twice. It had been mailed back to her from a hotel on Mackinac Island once, and also, she had left it at her cousins' house in Dearborn. But that was when she was younger.

The arboretum was a great place, because it was always free and always changing. Also, it was open every day of the week. What could be better? Aref and his parents went often. Aref pretended it was his backyard.

The arboretum was next to a railroad track and a river. Walking around in nature, anywhere, you could imagine the whole world was at peace.

Aref's class had also hiked over to the arboretum one day when they were learning about plants. They were going again later in

the spring when the peonies came into bloom. The Nichols Arboretum boasted one of the world's great peony gardens! People drove in from all over Michigan, and even Ohio, to see it. Aref didn't know what a peony was.

"A frilly flower with a lot of petals," Ms. Sullivan had said when he asked her. "A very special fancy flower with different tones of pink, sometimes white. You'll have to get one for your mother. In season, the grocery store sells them, or the farmers market, from big buckets."

Aref couldn't wait to see flowers that people would drive a hundred miles for.

At the arboretum they walked across Dow Prairie. It was the biggest page of snow yet. Aref and Layla ran and twirled. She threw

herself down on the ground and made a snow angel. Aref dug both his arms into a huge mound, then wrote "OMAN" with a stick in the snow.

Aref's father took a deep breath and stretched his arms out to either side. "I never knew I could like a real winter this much."

"I love it!" yelled Aref. He was kicking snow up with his boots, watching it fan in poufs.

"We had never been this cold before," said his father, laughing. "And it woke us up!"

Inside one of the greenhouses, they came upon a fragrant herb garden, each delicate plant in the raised beds neatly labeled: lavender, chocolate mint, spearmint, oregano. Layla stuck her face into a rosemary bush and said, "This one is the best!"

Aref's mother was fingering a few leaves of thyme. She said, "This is what my grandma used to cook green beans with, *ahhhh-hhh.*" She pinched her thumb and forefinger together and sniffed.

Aref's father had his head in the mint. He said, "Let's plant some chocolate mint at home on our patio when spring comes."

And an idea popped into Aref's head. He would turn his terrarium into an herb garden instead of a turtle prison. He could put it near his window. The glass would shine in the sunlight. It would be easy to water. He would just need some dirt. He already had the garden tools, from helping with the plants on the patio. Pebbles under the dirt would help the water drain. He would take care of his herbs and pinch off little bits and leave them in the

kitchen. He would share some with Hugh. He would be an herb farmer by summertime!

As they were leaving the arboretum, they passed the gift shop and Aref looked through the window. There, stacked up inside, were bags of very nutritious soils for house plants and some herbs in pots lined up just waiting for him!

He and Layla chose three pots each. The lady at the counter gave them each a bag to carry their purchases in. Aref's dad carried the dirt. Aref was a farmer by the time he got home.

Dear Sidi,

Tonight I planted some herbs. You like herbs.

We ate falafel sandwiches that were so big I could only finish half.

A lot of things are huge here.

I will be able to put my own mint leaves in lemonade soon.

Remember when you used to do that?

Guess what, I planted them where the turtle was supposed to live!

Did I tell you I am not getting a turtle after all? It is okay. I know where they are.

Love,

Aref

Sidi Changes His Mind

One lovely Thursday, after many days without talking to anyone, Sidi decided to go down to the souk, in the old city of Muscat, to walk among the shops.

He would stride along cobbled alleyways and smell the smoldering frankincense, admire the pretty folded rainbow-colored cloths and stitched hats and glittering little lamps, and have a few tiny cups of coffee or tea with his old friends. Yes!

Back when Sidi ran his own shop that sold sandals, he used to do this all the time. At lunch, after work, it was his personal neighborhood then. Everybody visited regularly, "smelled the air," shared the news. Sidi needed to see his friends. If the sultan could die, anyone could die.

Sidi parked Monsieur, his trusty old jeep, on a side street, climbed out, and headed toward the souk. Just walking there made him think of being young.

In those days his wife was still alive and Aref's daddy and his brother were still little boys running around the house.

When you are young, you are fairly certain you will always be young.

Sidi stepped up the ancient curb, heading straight through the lovely floating fragrance

in the air toward Ali's Palace of Brocade. This was the place many women came when they were planning to get married. They would buy beautiful cloths for their wedding dresses and to cover their tables. Other people came here to buy material to make pillows or curtains. Giant bolts of red and golden fabric were still standing up proudly inside Ali's doors. The shelves were still stuffed.

Sidi stepped into the crowded shop's interior.

"Have any cloth left for me?" Sidi called out in Arabic. Ali was bent down behind the counter, checking his telephone. He looked up in surprise.

"My friend!" he shouted. "I thought you had blown away on the far seas! Where on earth have you been? Where have you been hiding out?"

Sidi smiled, stepped into the shop a little shyly and kissed his friend Ali on both cheeks. They hugged very tightly. "I was just at home watching the sky change colors, what about you?"

"I've been here the whole time," said Ali.

Sidi nodded.

They hugged again. They sighed. They were quiet together for a moment. Sidi felt so glad to see someone he knew.

"Oh wait, that's not quite true," said Ali. "I haven't been here the *whole* time. I went to California!"

"You did?" Sidi was surprised. "California? Why?"

"To see my daughter! Did you know she and her husband moved to California?" asked Ali.

"You *went*?"

Ali raised his eyebrows. "Of course I went. Why not? Why do you look so surprised?"

"Who ran your shop?"

"I closed it for three weeks! The world didn't end!"

Ali was already heating the water in a silver samovar on his little burner, stirring the tea in, and arranging the tiny cups on a tray as people in Oman and the entire Middle East had been doing for thousands of years. The center of the wheel of days, the heart of the story. Someone visits you and you serve them.

"No sugar for me," said Sidi, raising one hand.

"Ah yes, I remember." Ali was pouring the tea into the cups. "You are my dear friend,

I would always remember that. And do you remember how much I like dates? In fact, I have some special plump ones. Here, have a date! The dates are sweet enough, who needs sugar?" Ali opened a shiny silver box and offered it. Sidi gently took one date. "But what about your family?" Ali asked. "How are they?"

Sidi shook his head. "They moved to Michigan. They are far away now, for three whole years." Sidi had settled into the old woven chair by the round brass table.

Ali placed a little cup in front of him and sat down across from him. "So when are you going to visit them?" he asked.

"Never! I can't fly."

"What? Why not?"

"I . . . don't know how."

"That's ridiculous! You sit in a seat, the same way you're sitting now. How hard can that be?"

Sidi said nothing.

"You don't have to fly the plane yourself! What is wrong with you?"

Sidi still said nothing.

"Are you worried about getting the tourist visa? I can help you. It's not that hard."

The tea was very hot. Sidi blew on it. He took the tiniest sip.

Ali was relentless. "The office is right up the street."

Sidi shook his head. "It would just be too difficult." He sighed. "I am a very old man."

"My friend! Nonsense! I remember you as a very brave and strong man. If you are brave, you don't get old. Why can't you get on

an airplane to see the people you love most? It would probably be a big help to *them* to have you show up!"

"What? Why?" Sidi had never thought of such a thing.

"I think your grandson would be overjoyed to see you. I bet he misses you. You deserve a trip, my friend. You can come back. I promise you, nothing will have moved."

Sidi didn't say a word. He didn't remember Ali being this bossy.

"Your house will still be there. Waiting for you."

Ali was also good at getting people to buy things. Apparently, he liked to talk others into action. Maybe it was his secret hobby.

"This tea is good. Have you sold anything today?" asked Sidi, trying to change the subject.

They sat in silence for a little while as two young women entered, fingered the silver fabric on the biggest bolt of cloth by the cutting table, and discussed their living rooms. Ali jumped up and offered to help them. They said they would be back, that they were just looking around now. Ali raised his hand pleasantly. “As you wish! Malish!”

He sat back down with Sidi. “Why not go?”

Sidi didn’t answer.

“Then when you come home, you are a traveler. You went to the other side of the earth. You have different pictures in your head. Like me right now, I have California in my head. I didn’t have it before.”

The shop was quiet for a long time.

“I would have Michigan,” Sidi finally said.

"Yes! Wherever that is, whatever it looks like, you would have it."

Another long silence.

"You have enough money for a plane ticket, right?" asked Ali.

Sidi laughed. "I think so. I don't know what they cost. I never buy much, so probably I do."

Ali stood up, collected their teacups, and picked up his keys.

"Come on, my friend. I am locking my shop right this minute and walking with you up the hill to the tourist agency. We are going to ask about the price of the ticket and get the form for the visa. You can take it home and fill it out, or I will help you right here."

Sidi shook his head.

He laughed out loud, suddenly.

Maybe Ali was right.

Maybe he could use a surprise in his own life.

He could change his mind.

They walked together up the hill.

Back and Forth

Sidi, where are you? Why aren't you writing me? We are so sad about Sultan Qaboos. I wish he lived longer. I couldn't believe it.

School is great. I think science is my favorite thing. We saw a video about eels and the Great Barrier Reef in Australia. My teacher went there. My best friends are Robin and Layla. Someday we are all going to go to Australia and take a glass-bottomed boat to see the coral under the water.

Love, Aref

DEAR AREF,

THANKS FOR YOUR LETTER!

SORRY I WAS SLOW TO WRITE, BUT NOW I CURED MY STOMACH.

I SHOULD HAVE LISTENED TO THE YOGURT FROM THE BEGINNING.

THE YOGURT WAS MY DOCTOR.

DID YOU KNOW I HAD A STOMACHACHE?

I HOPE YOU WILL NEVER HAVE A STOMACHACHE.

BUT IF YOU DO, JUST REMEMBER THIS ONE THING—

YOGURT!

LOVE,

SIDI

Sidi, that is funny about yogurt.

The snow here is softer than a pillow.

It was asking about you.

Ha ha! That sounds like something you would say.

Love,

Aref

AREF, I HAVE A BIG SURPRISE FOR YOU.

IT IS THE BIGGEST SURPRISE EVER.

YOU WILL NEVER GUESS.

BUT SOON YOU WILL KNOW.

LOVE,

SIDI

Dear Sidi,

What what what?

You have to tell me!

Love,

Aref

DEAR AREF,

I CAN'T.

THEN IT WOULDN'T BE A SURPRISE.

LOVE,

SIDI

Pet Poems

Ms. Sullivan brought her dachshund Wally to school one day. In the classroom she unhooked his little blue leash. Wally ran around sniffing everybody, then lay down under Aref's desk, at his feet.

"He likes you best!" Jameela said.

Aref was surprised. He missed Mish-Mish, his orange cat in Oman, very much, so this made him happy.

That day they were writing poems about pets—pets you had now, or used to have, or wished you could have. Jameela wrote about her canary Cheepers who flew away, but then came back again! Cheepers was sitting on their porch railing two days later when she came home from school. Other people made things up.

My dreamy elephant Escarole
curls his trunk into a circle,
I climb on, lie down,
and he lifts me high
above his head
where I sleep all night.
You have different dreams
in an elephant's trunk.
They smell like peanuts.

—by Mahmoud

Tony the Tarantula

guards my room.

No one will come in if he is sitting there.

Some people scream if they see a tarantula,

but I like his fuzzy legs and his smile.

—by Kojo

Aref wrote about how Mish-Mish used to sleep in his sock drawer, or on Aref's bed, on top of his feet. Mish-Mish felt like he weighed fifty pounds at night. Aref didn't make anything up.

The World Is Wide and . . . Who Are You?

Sidi thought about wearing Western clothes for the long journey. Of course he had some. He had one outfit. A jacket even. Many younger men in Oman wore pants and T-shirts and jackets instead of dishdashas and stitched hats or turbans. Aref and his dad had always worn Western clothes.

Sidi tried on his brown pants. They had deep pockets. He tried to wear them for a

whole afternoon instead of his usual clothes. But he didn't like the way they felt. He didn't like wearing a belt. He put on his regular clothes again, climbed into Monsieur, and drove back down to the Old City.

When he entered Ali's Palace of Brocade, he saw his friend on the floor, cutting some cloth with big scissors. "What are you doing?" he asked Ali.

Ali looked up. "Sewing a pillow."

"You can sew?"

"Of course I can sew! I am a cloth man! Who did you think makes the displays in my window?"

Sidi shrugged. "I didn't know that. I'm impressed. I have a question. Can I wear my regular clothes in the airplane?"

"You can wear anything you want!" said

Ali. "You could even wear your pajamas under your dishdasha! I did."

"Really?"

"Sure. Who cares?"

"I wouldn't want to do that."

"But you sleep on the plane, so you want to be comfortable! And then, you don't have to pack them!"

"Maybe I'll just wear my pajamas with three dishdashas on top and won't have to pack anything. What do you think?" said Sidi.

"Fine! Suit yourself! Ha! You're not a movie star. No one cares about your clothes." Ali bit off a long red thread and waved his needle in the air.

Sidi smiled. He wanted to remain an Omani in the sky. He didn't like the idea of looking unidentifiable in Western clothes, up above the clouds.

Flying Thoughts

Sidi packed his jacket and his Western clothes (just in case) in his very little suitcase. He took a toothbrush and his comb. He remembered Aref having a hard time packing. Why? You didn't need much. But Aref had been moving away for three years, and Sidi was only visiting.

He took a taxi to the airport, walked gingerly into that glittering glass world, and before he knew it, was in a wheelchair since Ali had insisted on it, so Sidi wouldn't get lost. This made him feel a little bad, since really he could walk just fine and he didn't want anyone to think he was just making them work hard to push him. But the nice young man pushing him didn't seem to mind. His name was Hisham. They chattered as they rolled along. Hisham asked him where he was going and why and told him he was lucky to be flying.

Sidi quickly realized that Ali had been right; it was a very good thing for him to be in a wheelchair right now, because he felt instantly overwhelmed by all the people and signs in this buzzing modern place, and he needed someone to take him to the exact right gate. He wondered what Aref had thought of

all these moving walkways and displays in front of shops. An airport was its own little world. He hadn't quite realized this. There was a bank and a medical room and a prayer room!

And so many beautiful, kind ladies and men, dressed up, not dressed up, smelling sweet, so many kids with their own little suitcases, pink princesses and scary dragon faces on them, so many bright lights and signs and purses and scarves, voices speaking different languages, such a fabulous crowd of comings and goings that Sidi never even dreamed about when he was sitting in his old stucco house by the lime tree.

When Sidi sat outside on his roof in the old metal chair and saw planes taking off, then flying high overhead into the night sky,

up there by the moon and the stars, he never thought about all this hustle and bustle at the airport. He was rooted on the ground, holding his prayer beads, staring up. And now here he was in the middle of the rush and the flow, sticking his hand into the deep pocket of his dishdasha to feel those beads again, to hold on to them for comfort. He said, “Hisham, I would have gotten lost without you!” Hisham laughed and said, “Don’t worry, we’ll get there!”

When they arrived at the gate, he said to Hisham, “I wish you a good life, my son! May you always find your way!”

Hisham thanked him for the tip.

Once Sidi was on the plane, in his own seat, confounded by all the levers and buttons that Aref had loved so much, and the man

beside him had shown him how to buckle his seat belt, and he had placed his little pillow securely behind his neck, on the first leg of flying to Kuwait, he closed his eyes.

He would not think about leaving the ground.

He didn't like it.

It was too much for him.

He would think about the Arabian leopard. Yes, perhaps there were only two hundred of them left in the world, but they were still proud, hiding out in the south of Oman among high desert cliffs and rugged mountains, finding food and water somehow, wearing their gorgeous polka-dotted coats, sneaking around in the dark. Now Sidi was like one, too, going somewhere in the dark.

He wasn't sure this was a good thing. People

should sleep in the dark—not fly around the world. But he wouldn't think about it. He would think about mysterious sinkholes fed by springs, full of secret turquoise water, the holes channeling deep, deep into the ground.

He would think about fat honey badgers, cute as skunks, with their own pale stripe down their backs, holding their tails up proudly, making a parade through the desert dunes.

The Arabian partridges hopping in circles, chattering in families, showing one another where the grubs were. He would think about the majestic sea turtles feeling tired and swimming more slowly as they neared the beach after their long, long journeys.

He would think about stretches of land where no people live, only animals. He had

seen the ibex running against an orange sunset.

He would think about birds rising up fearlessly from the branches of trees, taking on the whole sky. Birds always seemed confident. Seagulls dipping and diving over the waves never looked scared or worried. Could he picture a scared face on a bird? No way.

He would not think about thick fog or even mist.

Shelter

Aref's parents told him a lie. But it was a good lie, a really really good lie, and later they would say it did not qualify as a lie. Just a surprise. They told him they had to go to the airport to pick up a professor.

"What is his name?" Aref asked.

He thought it seemed strange when neither of them answered.

At the Detroit airport, a million people

were still coming and going. Aref and his parents didn't know any of them. They stood at the end of a long hallway waiting.

They were not looking for anyone in a wheelchair. So when the wheelchair rolled through the crowd carrying a familiar man in a bright white dishdasha, gleaming and smiling, they were tongue-tied and stunned. Aref couldn't believe it. He looked at his mother and his father, a question in his eyes. Was this the surprise Sidi had been talking about?

Aref's father kneeled down next to Sidi. "Are you okay? Why are you in a wheelchair?"

Sidi waved his hand. "Ali insisted." He gestured to the young woman pushing his chair. "Meet my new friend Emma! My kind host!"

Emma smiled shyly at them. She said, "Nice man!"

Sidi handed Emma a rolled-up blue bill with the face of the sultan printed on it. "I am sorry I don't have any American money yet," he said.

She stared at the bill with wonder. "This is amazing!"

"Yes, it is very beautiful. Keep it for your collection."

Aref was whooping, jumping up and down. He was clapping his hands together saying, "No way, no way! You all tricked me!" He was bouncing around Sidi as Sidi stood up and started to walk, stiffly at first, alongside him, trying to hug him and hold his hand all at once. Sidi—no way—Sidi had tears running down his cheeks.

This was what happened! People came to America and they cried!

"You came, Sidi! This is too great! See, it wasn't hard, right?" said Aref.

"Oof! That Paris airport!" Sidi was laughing, too, with relief. "Sorry I'm so stiff. I'll stretch out in a minute."

"Now you are a falcon!" said Aref.

It was hard to walk with so much hugging and crying going on. Aref's mother had brought one orange rose all the way to the airport for the professor, she said. Now she handed it to Sidi. He held it between two fingers and kissed everyone on both cheeks.

As they drove toward Ann Arbor, Sidi's eyes were wide. "Yes, yes," he said. He kept turning his head to look out of both sides of the car. He liked the signs and the barns.

Aref leaned against his shoulder in the

backseat. Sidi still smelled like orange water and stones.

"Let's take a walk and I will show you everything," said Aref.

"*Everything*," said Sidi.

When Sidi unpacked his suitcase, he had one smooth, white stone, as flat as a little tabletop, tucked in between his neatly folded white undershirts. "Here you go," he said, handing it to Aref. "It is the table of the Omani mouse."

Making Friends

Sidi said he thought he'd sleep for a few days first. He was sleeping on the couch, which Aref's parents had opened into a bed. They had bought him a new orange blanket. But really he only slept for a few extra hours, plus the night.

He kept staring at all of them and smiling, drinking little cups of tea, then standing at the front window staring out into the parking

lot. "It's a different world!" he said. "But not that different."

They took him on a drive around Ann Arbor so he could see Aref's school and the university and the shops and restaurants. They drove out into the country to Independence Lake and walked on the beach. As usual, Sidi bent over and picked up stones. He took deep breaths and said, "It feels calm here. I thought it might feel more crowded."

Hugh and the Finnegans and Hayan and Layla's family came for a big dinner. The apartment was *stuffed*, and everyone had fun and told stories and asked a lot of questions. Sidi and Hugh were instant best friends.

So Many Flavors

On Grandparents and Special Friends Day Sidi visited Aref's classroom and met everybody. They lined up to shake his hand, and Petra curtsied to him, as if he were the queen of England. There were other grandparents there, too. Marielena's abuela had brought a piñata stuffed with candy, Dahlia's yaya delivered large plates of Greek cookies covered in powdered sugar, but

Sidi was the star since he had traveled so far to get there. He said, "Greetings, you citizens of the country with so many flavors." He had just seen a sign for an ice cream called Frosted Blueberry Animal Cookie Dough and thought it sounded funny.

Ms. Sullivan loved him instantly. Aref could tell. She seated him in her soft story time chair. She said, "I am coming to Muscat someday."

Sidi smiled. "Ahlein! Welcome!" he said.

Dahlia, Kojo, and Joaquin and some of the other kids adopted Sidi immediately since their grandparents lived too far away to come to school. They liked his dishdasha. They liked his sandals. He was wearing them with striped socks he had borrowed from Aref's father. He told them his favorite story about

the donkey and the cooking pans. Everybody ate cookies and drank apple juice from little boxes. Sidi asked Ms. Sullivan about her own grandparents. He said, "Tell us some stories." She said they had always dreamed about going back to a thatched-roof cottage in Ireland like their ancestors had lived in. Her great-great-great grandfather used to catch oysters in a net before coming to the United States. Sometimes oysters were eaten raw, and sometimes they were baked with a little white cheese on top. Ireland was rainy and cold, with fireplaces inside the cottages. But her grandparents? They had lived in the city of Detroit. They ran a shoe repair shop. They loved crusty bread and cheese.

Then they all talked about cheese. Dahlia told a story about her grandfather on a Greek island making white cheese for everybody. Marielena's abuela said she could make special white cheese enchiladas and bring them to school someday. Sidi said he could make cheese in a clean sock. Mahmoud asked Sidi in Arabic if he had ever been to Morocco and seen the olive pressers making olive oil, and Sidi answered in English, "Maybe I'll go there next. Why not?"

Jameela asked him if he was one hundred years old.

Sidi laughed and said, "Almost."

When Aref and Sidi were back in the apartment that afternoon, they sat in a circle with Aref's parents, telling stories about the great school visit. Aref's father said what Sidi used to say, "The house is happy now. It is really laughing." He turned to Sidi and

said, “I understand you have a lot of fans!” Ms. Sullivan had told him this when he was picking up Aref and Sidi. “Should we take a quick walk before dinner and all go out tonight instead of cooking? Sidi’s choice of restaurant! After all, it’s still Grandparents Day!”

Sidi chose Thai. He loved noodles a lot.

For the Moment

On Saturday the sun was blazing brightly. Only tiny lines of snow remained in the ditches by the road.

"Can I show Sidi where the turtles live, please?" Aref was pulling Sidi toward the front door by the hand. "It's warm enough now. Some might be out. Maybe we can find a Blanding's turtle that lives to be seventy!"

"My turtle brother!" said Sidi, laughing.

Aref's parents agreed so they bundled into the car and drove to where their favorite trail began. No other cars were in the parking lot yet—it was a very quiet Saturday morning. The giant trees of Michigan rose up into the sky on both sides of the path. Sidi lifted his face. He was staring up into the branches and smiling. He said, "Beauty! Pure beauty! The leaves are a screen for the light. Look!" Then he started walking carefully with one hand on his hip, stretching his legs, and asked, "How do you know those turtles are still there?"

"Turtles are trusty, remember?" said Aref. "They come back. They like swimming around a big broken root sticking out of the water. We might not see all the kinds—really the Blanding's is rare—but maybe we can

see an eastern box, or a wood turtle. I would really like to see the spiny softshell with the pig nose. Some of them hibernate when it's cold. But they shouldn't be laying their eggs yet, not till May. That's when they go to the fields."

"Hmm," said Sidi. "We can always count on turtles."

Even though Aref and Sidi were walking slowly, Aref's parents had fallen behind and were stooping to look at some moss. Aref's father was stepping back to photograph it. Probably he would research it later. He was pocketing a pine cone or two, gently brushing off the dirt.

"I'm so glad you came, Sidi!" said Aref.

Sidi squeezed his hand. "I am glad, too!" he said. "Who would have guessed I could fly

just like a falcon? I went halfway around the world to find you again."

Birds chirped in the branches. Their little bell voices bounced back and forth.

"Yes, you did! Here I am!" said Aref.

Sidi continued, "Everything changed when I did that one new thing. I thought flying was only for other people, but it turned out I could do it, too."

"Doing new things is good for the brain," Aref said. "That's what Ms. Sullivan told us."

"My brain? Happy," said Sidi.

"Let's go to a factory soon and see an assembly line," said Aref. "Or we can go to that island without any cars. Or see a bear!"

"Maybe today!" said Sidi.

Trail Talk

Sidi: The earth in the United States smells like grass and mud and snow and rain.

Aref: Sidi, if you didn't come, nobody at school would have gotten to meet you.

Sidi: I am now an international star.

Aref: Ha ha. Sidi is a moonbeam.

Sidi: Aref is a good trail guide.

Aref: So how long can you stay? You haven't told us. Can you stay for three years like we will?

Sidi: Ha ha! My visa—you know what that is? It's my ticket to get into this country—a visitor visa—says I can stay six months. But I thought I would stay three.

Aref: Why not six?

Sidi: Six is half of a year. My house will be crying. Three only. Even three months is very long. You stay three years, I stay three months. Maybe I could come back next year?

Aref: Really? Please!

Sidi: Ha ha! We'll see. I think it's a good idea.

Sure enough, the turtles were in their same spot, even after that snowy winter, dipping, diving, sunning on a log, staring out at the day.

"See!" said Aref, pointing. "Look for one

with a bright yellow throat; that might be a Blanding's."

"The turtles are little," Sidi said.

"They're not *that* little."

"Compared to our turtles back home, I mean."

"Every turtle is little compared to those," Aref said. "And isn't it great? That I didn't take one?"

Sidi looked at him. "You were going to take one from here?"

Now Aref felt embarrassed that anyone had ever had that thought. "It was Mom's idea. But I said no. People aren't supposed to take turtles from the wild. I'm growing mint instead."

"*Hmm.* Because anyway, you can visit them." Sidi was stepping over some stones and

roots, leaning down closer to the water. Two red sliders were paddling in circles. No rare turtles today. "So, they're all yours anyway."

"Right! I didn't think of that," said Aref.

Sidi put his arm around Aref and hugged him tightly.

"We are both Michiganders now," Aref said.

"What?"

"That's what they call people here."

"Ah! Yes, we are," said Sidi, snapping a stick in two. "We are forest people. The desert people in the forest. For the moment."

"For the moment!"

Aref thought about that. He liked this moment. It would change. But he would remember it. He liked it almost as much as he had liked all his moments in Muscat. Now

he and Sidi had been in two different homes together. And they both felt good. They had shared a million moments. There could be more than one home. Friends and neighbors and beds and windows and skies and moons in all of them. Someday they would both be back in Muscat again, riding around in Monsieur the jeep, remembering this.

"Sidi," Aref whispered, pointing. "That turtle is looking at you!"

Acknowledgments

Gratitude to Virginia Duncan; Paul Zakris; Lois Adams; Tim Smith; Greenwillow Books; Eliza Fischer; Rand and Beth Brandes; the truly wonderful "Little Read" program at Lenoir-Rhyne University (Hickory, North Carolina); the enthusiastic children of North Carolina; Wesley Hall Furniture; Ron and Sandra Deal; Jonathan Ray; Caroline Webster; Rohinie Silva; Paige Spilles; Ryan Callaway; Chris Hays; Josephine Weissberg; Frankee Liddy of Belfast, Northern Ireland, who said, "The turtle is always at home;" the American International School of Muscat (TAISM); *My Heart Is Not Blind,* by Michael Nye; and Martin Luther King Jr. Elementary School, Ann Arbor, Michigan.